River & the Taʌı

No proper introduction or contents page, I've avoided using chapters as they annoy me when I read and I think they are a waste of time, I've split this journey into 3 parts, you'll know exactly when they are, the 2nd is obvious and the third one will be obvious once you're a few pages in.

In short the book as it says on the blurb is essentially a mix of all the media I love—put into a book, consistent inconsistency…lines…breaks…pauses…gaps—
indifferent to the taste of others, regardless—it is my soul on paper

Shout out to all of the people around me that have allowed me to be myself.

Particular shout outs to:
Cameron Scrimgeour
Lilly Blackwood
Jack Kerouac
Allen Ginsberg
Jerry Garcia & Grateful Dead
Ksenija & Branko Raseta
Betty
Christopher Hitchens

Alright, I'll give it a go— it might be a show.
Taxi, I want to go home.
"Well, Do you want to go home or shall I take you for a ride?"
The taxi man said, sensing my apprehensive stride through language.
"I don't really mind, I just don't want to go to bed"
"I'd take you home but even you don't know where that is, if you can show me the road, i'll carry you home to rest your weary head…i guess"
"I don't know where my home is"
"I don't know where I'm going…and quite honestly I'm tired of going…coming, going. Now you see it now you don't, what is it? Like, really? WHAT is IT?" River says with a very strong tone, almost a passionate autistic type energy.
"I don't know man you're getting a little heavy, I'm just a taxi driver, I don't hold any answers other than the names of the roads around here and maybe a little trivia i've picked up over the years, so again where do you want to go?
"I already said man. I don't know, maybe just drive around, keep the metre running, it doesn't matter, I just want to be nowhere, and if you can leave me in peace I'd appreciate that."

“Well”
Said the taxi man looking back at River through the rear view mirror over his obviously fake Gucci sunglasses with the crossbar on top, Dahmer style the interior mirror not the side ones, “that's gonna cost you a whole lot, are you sure? There's a forest nearby, I could take you there? Or if we turn on the next junction I can take you to the hills where you can glare at the moon”
“Nah man that’s too cliche, and what am i gonna when i get there? Sit under a tree until I get enlightened like the Buddha or just freeze to death in the perilous cold, look I don’t want to be rude man but I want to break out of my mould, not sink deeper into it, its rigid like an old railway bridge and i’m loose like jelly, I just don’t fit”
Again, autistic tones from River.
“Okay, okay man, I’ll just drive. If you like any kind of scenery let me know, though it is dark so you can’t see anyway”
“Yeah, I don’t need to see really, what is there to see anyway, I’ve seen it all before, like I said, I don’t want to be anywhere, and where can you go when you don’t want to be anywhere you know?”

“I do know and probably why I drive a taxi and have for the last 25 years, I drive from place to place picking people up, picking their stories up, I’m almost like a human energy collector, everyone who passes through leaves a little something for me you know? and it’s as if my whole life has been in this taxi, its my operating system, it's my home, I too like, being nowhere because really it's everywhere, the places you see, the people you meet, It’s all just you and me my friend, we might as well be up in the galaxy in a floating drive-through diner with some kind of space coffee and even better Wine, ahh, what goes on down here is always going on either way so you need not question it, you can be in 2 places at the same time you know?
Think about God”
“God?, huh, tell me about God”
“Well I just did but I can’t right now as God evades words, as a great zen master once said, you can only hit me when you don’t try to, any desire to encapsulate God pushes God away, those who speak do not know, those who do not speak, know. So, we must find a way of speaking without knowing”
Man, all you God people are the same, it's all mystical and beyond what we can conceive, why think about it if it evades words? Thoughts? Feelings? Isn’t it just a big waste of time? A search for what?

You're better off searching for gold, at least you may find some.
"That right there is the start of your awakening or…i mean you've probably been thinking about this for a while so I'll take back the condescending tone; I apologise, questioning your reality is good, it shows intelligence, marks that you can think for yourself, and don't look at it as searching but rather receiving, once you're open to the universe, to God, to your divine self, once you surrender the rest is taken care off for you"
Hey would ya take a right down there i think it leads to a cool castle, feel like I've been here before, hmmm.

My heads in the clouds

Help me come down
Feel the ground, for you ground me,
Ever ever so soundly

Presently my he- my heart is pounding
LOUDLY
Ever expanding and
Unsure of a safe landing

And so

I'll stay standing

though

There is nowhere to stand

“Are you sure? That leads to Folkestone and Dover, it's a bit of a drive to that castle your talking about, you must have been here before if you know about the castle, it is a pretty thing, little bit disappointing after hiking all the way up there and you kinda just look at it then walk away, turning back every few moments as a kind of mark of respect because you’re leaving it so soon and you’re trying to show the universe that you do care but really you couldn’t care less; otherwise you’d carefully observe the bricks, form a layman's theory about when its from and maybe even google it, sorry, my brain does that to me sometimes and I give in everytime.”

Yeah, yeah lets go, I know where we are actually, it's quite a view-

River is cut off as the taxi pulls into a Jet petrol station, where on earth did he find this? Pre-war Sarajevo? No wait, we're on the south coast of England.

“Hey, do you want anything? I’m guessing we’re not stopping anytime soon so you’d better stock up on…something? Do you drink? Do you want a beer or two, four? Or coffee if that’s your thing, we’ll go over to the rest stop for a cigarette, you can’t smoke here”

Oh yeah, petrol and flames and that, yeah, uhhh you know what could you get me some kind of merlot, paprika crisps, but uhhh crinkled, I prefer how they keep the flavour, salt and vinegar as well as it goes with the wine, and 2L of water.

I only know me when i know you, it's only through you I see my own divinity
And the peace from within wettens and softens the hard edges of our minds.
Peace will come when all hate is gone
but this old world with never change

The way it's been
We're all searching for something, but let it not be Dolphins
Though they're beautiful,
Let it not be Dragons too
Though they're ethereal

I think we and our cats want something a little bit more real
A basic meal like bread and water
A ' I Love you' with sincere eyes
And such a smile we have to look away and almost deny
But deep inside we know we are loved
For there is nothing else we can do for one another

River watches the driver walk out the car, and notices the man's strange attire, 3 people in line before him, a large-lady's got her weekly shop, haribos, 5 microwave meals, all different kinds, picky kids? Or just a chaotic household, yeah probably. Why do people dress as if other people can't see the- oh he's back, say, you're dressed quite strange, but well, for an older guy, I was just thinking about people disregarding an aesthetic way of being, not for other people but for yourself you know? And maybe you'll inspire other people to do the same, nah I don't know.

"No no that's a good point, you have to look at yourself and everything around you everyday, you might as well make it beautiful, but also at one point you come to realise that everything is beautiful, still though, it's a kind of respect to yourself to present your "character" as you desire, along with other aesthetic pleasures.

What did you get for yourself?

River enquiries, leaning in over the quite frankly dusty headrest, unusual for a taxi, the COVID screen had been removed too, which I think is actually illegal, I like it.

"I got the wine and crisps, got us a 12 pack of 500ml waters, and I just got a double box of cigarettes for myself"

Oh, what did you go for?

"Marlboro gold, the perfect cigarette"

The driver looks back making a rather European kind of smirk.
“Yeah I can't fault you for that.”
The Driver pulls out of the petrol station and notices the rest stop is only on the other side of the motorway, “Ah fuck it, shall we just smoke them in here?”
Wow, you’re my kind of taxi driver, yeah sure, light up man, would it be too much to ask if I could smoke a joint in here? I was gonna ask earlier but I didn’t want to push it and I assumed we were gonna stop a bunch anyway.
“I mean, it doesn’t look like this car is going back into the depot anytime soon, so why not, make sure the cameras don’t see you tho- It’s getting dark anyway actually it doesn’t matter, you know this route is heading straight for Dover right, there's not much in that town, as you probably know.
“Yeah even so, let’s go.”

I'm wasting so much time and i can't stop myself from doing so
The negativity of my words will not cease
Even if i want them too
And it's all in my mind
But why shall i battle
When is it all loss?

Should I not just concede?
I cannot carry on
The way i've been

This new breath of fresh air is really smoke
And its killing me slowly
Rather than at my own rate

It's been exactly 10 years of pondering
I'm wasting so much time and i can't stop myself from doing so
I can't feel better I was born sick
People should be happy

Not writing sad poems to perform to strangers and one divine...

There's that long winding road that takes you from Dartford all the way to Dover, and you can see the port long before you arrive, seagulls screaming, waves crashing, vehicles from all over, angry Romanian truck drivers being pulled over before boarding due to being obviously overweight, I mean not obvious to me but those officials really know what they're doing.
“So, do you wanna turn back around or go up the east coast towards Newcastle or?”
No no, just keep driving.
“If we keep driving we'll end up in France, or Holland..”
Yeah I mean just keep driving, we'll see where we end up.
“You should probably put that joint out now, is that your second one? I didn't even see you roll that, we'll be at the border soon, is it a coincidence that you had your passport with you already and a bag with what I gather is clothing and maybe a laptop, you look like the type”
Yeah, clothes, no, no laptop, the large bulge is an Udu drum, it was the only one I could fit in my bag and I didn't want to bring THE BIG BAG, you know.
“oh , of course your a musician, i'm surprised you haven't asked me to put the radio on”
Yeah, that being said, could you put something bluesy on? Do you have any Clapton? That'll make my soul sing, Lay Down Sally? Rest here in my arms, don't you…sorry, love that song.

“Uhh no but I've got the unplugged album? That’s a classic right, or use spotify if you want”

Nah just leave it on shuffle man it's all good stuff.

“So, you’re paying for the Ferry right? Were you expecting this or what? It’s quite a risk to just call a taxi and expect them to drive you...nowhere? To France? To Austria? How exactly will you know you’ve arrived, and when we get there will we just drive back? Or what? This is gonna be very expensive for you, i’m not even sure how I have faith that you will pay for this but I somehow just went along with it, maybe I also want that sense of adventure”

This isn’t even “adventure” I just have no choice really, I guess it's an adventure in an off-handish way, I’m just curious you know, where will we end up? Where will my mind end up? Is it all the same? Will I return to Luton with the same feeling I set off with or will it be something entirely different? I think it's probably, you know what nah, no i wanna get out, i can’t just drive around as a passenger on my own journey it's just not right,it was right for the time being but hmmm i don't know i think i should just walk, you know what give me your number, this has been profound but i need to be alone now and even though you’re cool and everything, i just need to be alone.

“Well, that’ll be £120, I did say it would add up, where will you go now? You have nothing booked and it's almost 11pm, its dark, cold, where will you go”
“It doesn’t matter”

River opens his door and walks slowly to the boot of the car, jordan lace untied, jesus man why did i wear these im gonna be fucking walking.

“Joined ignorance

Ignorance is not an option, we all must learn otherwise no one goes, people are swallowing numbers as if its gonna save them from their putrid minds, we’re nothing without our mothers and our environment, we must change before we change our environment for the environment will not change us, I cannot see without my glasses but I can see and hear clearer, if you’re like me you’ve hit a brick wall and have nowhere left to turn.

The world will not open

When all we want to do is climb”

Well, here I am, I don't know where I am or where I'm going, do I just sit or do I mindlessly walk and will the decision make any difference at all? I think I'll walk, at least it gives the illusion of stuff happening, stuff, you know, cars and all that, people talking at you when you can't make out what they're saying but they keep going and going, forward and forward, at you despite of your reluctance in your fake smile, oh man can you not read body language. That hotel in the centre of Dover? I think I can probably do better but I've seen it so many times and it must look as bad inside as it does out? No, no i'll keep walking, man i've done this so many times and it always just gets too cold and I always end up overpaying for a really bad sleep, really it's the shower that hits and the 2 instant coffees i chain before being rushed out at an unreasonable latest check out time, just another hour honestly, that's all, I like a long shower and I like to clean the room a little bit, i'm not an absolute slob.

“Okay, so if I'm just quiet I can stay back here? I'll just read, don't worry, just let me know when we're in France, or…wherever we're going ""Yes, Yes, no worry” The man replies in a thick Albanian accent, “And you? Where are you coming from?

You're not British with this moustache" "Hahaha, yeah, ex-Yugoslavia" I said, "Well spotted, wherever I go the people accept me as their own, Turkey, Egypt, Bosnia, well.."You okay with me, i'm okay with you, you know" The mans says quite sympathetically, "I know the tension between our countries, but we're just humans, do you agree? I'm sure you do, you wouldn't have approached me otherwise, there were plenty of Romanians, Bulgarians, maybe even Serbs, you could have asked; it's almost as if you wanted something a little different; and I respect that, are you sure you can stay quiet back here? It is 2 and a half hours?"

"Honestly man don't worry about it, you're saving me loads, i've got water and a lamp, i'll be alright" I say at a speed to reassure him, absolutely nice man, I look forward to hearing what kind of life he's had, I wonder where the taxi has got to? He did leave his number.

It's very dark back here, I've always wondered what it would be like to get smuggled across a border, a serious one I mean, I've ridden in the back of a logging lorry with an illegal amount of alcohol, cigarettes...and a few logs, the flap kept lifting up but I guess if they caught us it wouldn't have been on me anyway, this time on the other hand. The human brain does weird stuff in darkness, how long have I been here?

I can hear water hitting the ramp thing, is it supposed to be coming onto the platform though? My good family friends once stayed in the car for the entire duration of a ferry trip and they said the same thing, I won't worry, I'm sure it's fine. God, I hope its France, I mean I won't know my way, either way but at least it's somewhat familiar, those complex tight turns upon entry in Dunkirk, "Calais - Left"
"Why am I here" River says loudly to himself, "I'm not even sure what country I'm in its so fucking dark, hey, hey, you speak Eng..." They're not even looking man nevermind, I'm going to assume its France from the travel time though really it could be anywhere, it's funny not really experiencing the time, it could be anything, like seriously anything, sometimes i zone out to such an extent i'm not sure if I am where my visual stimuli is leading to believe but i guess it's just important to keep going.

God, I'm really hungry. I should've packed something, I'm going to be walking for a while, man my feet already hurt, was this a good idea? I'm gonna call the taxi when I get to a petrol station though I could just do the same thing here? I don't think they'll be as understanding as in England though, how strange of a person do you have to be to allow someone to just...drive around with you, without a direction in mind, it's peculiar we ended up in Dover though, maybe he did it on purpose.

02:00

I'm just gonna have to walk through the night I have no other option, I didn't even bring a tent, luckily I have an astounding 220 euros to my name, I should be able to get any old tent for 20, a pot to cook in for free maybe even, yeah I'll look for cheap kitchen or camping joblots on facebook marketplace that should do the trick— I wonder how much I could earn busking, maybe I could even stay in a hostel when its too wet, my feet are already drenched; this is going to be a recurring theme and I'm not looking forward to it; when your whole bodies soaked you kinda just get on with it, you can't do much about it...I'll sell the Jordans to some kind of streetwear rat..uh hooligan...uh, youth? That's me as well but I don't need Jordans. I need walking shoes, something comfortable at least, why didn't I think about this before setting off. They're half a size too big and I'm wearing normal socks, even with boot socks they're a little clumsy.

I already know its a hell of a trek to Paris from here, I'd better go to Lille first I think that's not too far, by the time I get there it should be morning and maybe I can hitch a ride to Paris or at least part way, no trucks though I don't think, there's something off about truck drivers, I only know that because I wanted to be a truck driver when I was little; and there's definitely something off about me otherwise I wouldn't be doing this.

Lille - 96km

Oh Jesus Christ man, and I thought I could walk to Paris…I won't even make it halfway by daybreak, what a delusional mind I have, "You've always been a dreamer River" Yeah I guess Nathan was right. Maybe I should head towards Spain after I get to Paris, there might be a bus or something, yeah I'll get a bus, yeah.

River gets to Saint-Omer at 8:45, where he meets a man in similar attire to himself, maybe he could take me closer to Paris, that is a tie dye though i'm not sure what sect of hippy he is, if he's a deadhead or an Allman bro i've hit the goldmine but that would be too good honestly, we could talk about music and how the worlds going to shit, that is a nice car, that's the exact one I want though he's gone for magenta rather than yellow, I like magenta.

It's one of my favourite colours though I keep that a secret like most of my favourite things; what's the use in people knowing ALL of your favourite things, you have to keep some to yourself otherwise people just project and trying telling you about your own taste, I don't need that, I don't exactly know who I am at 24 years of age but I have a faint idea of my taste, you know.

"Hey, bonjour, do you speak English"

"Yes yes but not very well, who are you? Nice outfit, did you stop me because of the t-shirt? Do you like Lynyrd Skynyrd too? Or do you need directions?"

Wow what a nice guy, how did he know, both are correct, what a trip, in every sense of the word and phrase.

"Hahahah yes i do like Skynyrd and yes I need directions but I was going to ask for your help, where are you from you don't sound French?"

"I am Portuguese, where are you heading? Do you Brits not start with your name?"

“Oh sorry sorry I was caught up in my own stuff, I am travelling from England, I took a taxi and asked him to just drive without saying where, and I ended up in Calais, I’ve walked all night and i’ve decided that I want to go to spain and my name is River, well nickname, It’s easy to remember and my real name is hard to spell and pronounce for most people”

“That is absolutely ridiculous, are you being serious? I love you man, what an idiot you have to be to do such a thing, I am also a misfit, or rebel, whatever you people call it, outcast, something like that, I am on a long drive from Guimaraes, I was actually heading to Scotland, I’ve heard great things no?”

“Oh, yes Scotland is absolutely insane, though I was hoping to ask you to take me in the other direction, but yes I would absolutely go to Scotland if I were you, the people are the nicest in the UK, it's one of the best accents i’ve ever heard though you won’t understand a word, and it has some of the prettiest scenery on earth you know, though you are from Portugal and it is stunning there too”

“You want ME to drive you into Spain? You picked me to ask? Because I am wearing a Skynyrd tie dye…”

“Yes and it’s 1974, one of the best years of music if not the..”

“Best? Yes it is the best year for music without a doubt, 73 comes close, 72, 1959, 67 and 69. But why would you think I would take that risk? Grateful Dead? Does that say, who are they? They must have released a great album in 1974 if that's your favourite year? What a weird thing that we have the same taste? Or maybe we do, yet I've never heard of them? Get in my car, play me a song and we’ll see where we end up, like you with the taxi”

“Really? Oh man fucking hell, I love you too, probably, we’ll see. Though don’t get me wrong i'm into girls”

“Yes me too, men just don’t cut it...we’re...animals, this is the only t shirt in own in fact”

“Wait what's your name?
“Guilherme, very classic name for a man in Portugal”

“Wow, i’ve never heard that one, does it mean anything or are you not the type of person to know that kinda thing”

“Every name has a meaning my friend, in English I guess it would be, the absolute protector, or resolute, something like this.”

“That’s very fitting considering the situation”

Guilherme unlocks his car and River realises he was correct, the BMW E30 was in fact his, cream leather interior, matching dashboard, with one of those CD / Music systems that Europeans seem to love.

“This is your car? This is one of my absolute favourites though I would have gotten it in Yellow as I think it suits it a whole lot more”

“Yes of course, it is my first and only car I will ever own or drive, never entered another car and I never will, well other than before this one, if I was the one getting driven, yes but magenta looks cool at night, and I like driving at night, you could call me a nightsman”

“Uhh that’s not what you’d call a person who likes being awake at night but I like it, i’m gonna take that, I’m also a nightsman in some regard though I do love the sunshine, hence the yellow maybe, it’s a very happy colour as well, I also love Green as it has the most shades and it’s just so…visceral you know.”

“God, you like talking about colours a lot, are you going to play a song or what? I can’t drive in silence, my friend.

Guilherme hands the unreasonably long AUX cable to River.

“Here you are bro, play a couple if you want, i’m curious to hear this band, as that tee is sick, what’s this song called? Is it from 1974? Live version?, okay okay you must know your stuff, you know how long the drive is to Spain?, brother, it is very long, though i’m sure you don’t mind or care, you have nowhere to be, me neither, I quit my job to travel and now i'm going back on myself, oh well, at least I have company, I get a little lonely, perhaps we can go to Scotland after or something.”

“Scarlet Begonias, it’s the first Dead song i play for everyone, no one has ever disliked it, even my friend who doesn’t like the bands vibe and yes I know it’s a long drive but imagine walking it, that walk killed me so i’ll probably pass out at some point, if you don’t mind, I recommend you keep the music playing though, a certain effect happens when you leave them on, they enter you the way I imagine God enters into the soul, body and mind of a Christian.”

“So you are not a Christian then if you say it that way?

“It’s a little bit complicated but I am sure you’ll understand, I have some kind of feeling of faith in the world, myself, other people; such as yourself. The fact this very situation is unfolding is proving my own faith to me, you know? I grew up a hard headed atheist though I never used it as a title, only when talking about religion, in school and such, it annoyed me that people believed in something so preposterous just for the sake of it, you know? Just because their parents did, or because they thought it was the safe option, just in case there is a God and heaven, I’d better believe in it so that I don’t go to hell, in case that exists as well, because if there is a heaven for good people there must also be an alternative for bad people, though it always confused me hearing that dogs don’t get into heaven, what did they do?”

“I get that, I do, I am a Christian myself though I am losing faith in God by the minute and day, I wouldn’t quite call myself a religious person or an atheist, but I like belonging to something, if you get that, you might not, there's something nice about it though i know religion has not always been a force for good, maybe I am just a spiritual person, though us hippies and side of society people have loaded that term also so it’s lost its meaning to me, I don't really think about it a whole lot anymore but it is an interesting aspect of the world you know? Why are we here? Just to play?

A lot of people seem to think it's just to work and drink on weekends, go on a silly holiday once or twice a year (if you can afford it) and drink 3 times the amount they usually do, if that's their thing then, okay but, there must be more to this reality, when you look at history that really is the case, the Egyptians, the Aztecs, or Mayans, i'm not sure what the term is...or even those ancient mystics in India, I think there still are mystics in India, what a strange place, I mean i've never been but from what I can tell...maybe we should find a way to get to India, i'm quite sure you've never been either, huh?"

"It's funny you say that about people, "most people" as I always say but then contradict myself by saying oh no i can't generalise but it does seem to be true, "Friday night and you're not going anywhere after? A man said to me recently, as if young people have to go from pub to pub, to club to festival, I don't think he could believe that my night did in fact end at 11pm or midnight, why would I want to stay out longer? The next day is a saturday but it doesn't mean I have to stay out until a ridiculous hour, and I just don't really feel comfortable with most people in my generation or the UK even.

I'm not sure about other places even though I've seen quite a bit of europe, I like a more chilled out atmosphere, when people are drinking, i'm just wondering when a fight will break out, even that man looked angry, deep in his eyes was a sense of not being there, and even deeper in his eyes was a deep feeling of sadness, drinking alone on a friday night, among young people supporting a local singer, our friend actually, what a voice she has, that's beside the point though, I'm not exactly full of direction or happiness but it makes me sad seeing stuff like that, could he not have brought a friend out? Does he not have friends? He was a taxi driver too funnily enough, I kind of laughed inside of my head in the moment he said that as I knew what the first part of this journey was"

"Not really there? What do you mean, how do you know he wasn't there, maybe that's his relaxed space, the way you have your own way of relaxing through what i'm guessing is music? And or Cannabis or some kind of drugs? Though I can tell from looking at you that you're reasonable, you don't use Cocaine, or amphetamine, or Heroin, God bless you if you do but I can tell you don't, you wouldn't be here if so. There probably is a use for it but I imagine it's strictly medical or those in desperate need to escape reality, and that's fine, it's here for a reason, I don't judge, though it's hard sometimes.

I love some cannabis myself, psychedelics even but it comes to a point where you realise it's all the same state really and it just keeps you in a certain place, though a nice mixture of THC and CBD and you can't really complain, if you do, well not *need* but you know what i'm trying to say, when you desire that kind of relief, and drinking is just, not really great for anyone, glass of wine on a birthday or a few 4.5% beers in the sun, or a 5% from a tap or however you say it in the UK, though I get the feeling that you're not British, you speak extremely well but you seem extremely separated from the Brits, and the UK, wherever you are from, or born, or whatever your parents are; you don't seem to really align with that either otherwise you would have told me already I think, that must be extremely strange as I am portuguese, my Father is and my mother is Brazilian, but her parents were portuguese so really she is too, and I feel like that is my home, even though I was born in Spain, I resonate with the people, the land and the culture, what culture do you feel most closely related to, well I don't really know how to word it my English isn't that great, I'm one of those people who learned it from Netflix and sports, among other things, i've never had a British friend though."

“Yeah no, I think you’re completely right, I don’t resonate with the British culture all too much though I do sound entirely British, even my mannerisms are British, and my Family is from Ex-Yugoslavia, we’re Serbian really, but it makes me feel weird when I say or think that so I prefer Yugoslavia, I wasn’t alive in its prime but it seemed like a very happy and much better place than what Serbia and Croatia did to it, and Slovenia by starting the break up of the thing. It’s strange and somewhat funny, peculiar to think a country or coalition of that many states, a strong force, broke up to be many weaker and poorer ones, you’d think they’d want to stay together, many many people died in that period and im quite ignorant because as I said I wasn’t around and I have to go off of what my parents and grandparents have told me, and what biassed news outlets have said, it is difficult to read that kind of stuff from British and American media as they are the ones who initiated the bombings of Serbia; through NATO, which is why we sought asylum in the UK, our only option, other than staying and potentially dying or being captured and murdered by the Croatian forces, which is also dying I guess but a different kind, or staying and living in a country with absolutely no economy. I don’t blame anyone, it’s everyone's fault, the Serbs, the Croats, Nato etc.”

“Wow, that’s heavy, yeah no wonder you don’t really know who you are, I wouldn’t either but I would just call myself Serbian for the ease, so you don’t have to explain the whole thing everytime, which I'm sure you do, it is interesting, very interesting. I have read a little about it myself and i’ve had friends from every which angle, it’s nice to meet a non macho, non-nationalistic Serb, I hope you don’t mind me calling you that, as it does seem like it’s the truth, and you look Serbian, a little bit Turkish really, but just a tinge, maybe even slightly Iranian if you picked up a bigger tan.

“Yeah I don’t mind really, but that's why I go by River now, it’s just simpler and I've always said I like going with the flow, like a river, and Buddhism was the first philosophy I got along with, so it makes sense, I think?”

“Yeah I agree, it suits you. What is your name though if I may?”

River sighs but breaks into a hearty laugh and smile

“Ilija, and my surnames Raseta, but the S is a SH sound in my language”

River pronounces his full name in Serbian

“Wow, that is much cooler than river, and much more unique and uncommon, I’d just stick with that if i was you but I understand the trouble and potential hatred you could receive, i’m guessing it is the name Elijah in English, or in Portugal we have Elias, im sure it is the same name, something to do with God no? Quite ironic considering you grew up an Atheist hahahaha.”

River and Guilherme break into a laugh and then silence as Jerry Garcia of the Grateful Dead goes into the solo of the song, 8 minutes in, Guilherme opens the windows either side as it reaching noon and the temperature has rocketed up unexpectedly, the wind is low to River’s relief as he dislikes that force, as a walker and cyclist he finds it annoying, it lessens progress and gives him a headache, very much like his mother, which he would deny because he never liked complaining, even when in pain

“God, what a lovely day, I wasn’t expecting this at all, the nice day, someone agreeing to take me to Spain, the synchronicity of the shared music taste, cannabis and even the car, i’ve never got to even sit in this car and it’s been my favourite for years, what an absolute treat” River Exclaims with an defining look of ecstasy on his face, grinning from ear to ear.”

Can we stop to get something to eat at some point soon, I've still not eaten since I left Luton, it's on me, I was going to pick up a few second hand items so I could cook on the go and sleep wherever but I bumped into you so I didn't get the time"

"For sure, I'm also hungry, I forget to eat all the time, I know a good place coming up but it is 40km still, it'll be worth it i promise, if you can't wait I understand, we can get some petrol station food, though I'll warn you, it isn't very good and it's the same price as what we can get at this little deli in Amiens, it's a small city, I passed through on the way here a couple days ago, I'm sure you'll like it, it's a river town, though France is full of great food so really we could stop anywhere, though I would like to show you it. Can you endure another 40k? For the best, overfilled baguette you've ever had? Maybe not the best coffee you've ever had, and don't worry I'll pay for it, I don't want to ask you if you're poor but you probably would have eaten a few times by now if you had a lot of money."

"I can wait, I'm sure it'll be worth it, and please let me pay, at least this one time, it's the least I can do, petrol is expensive and you've been more than nice, this is way more than I was expecting from this experience, though I wasn't expecting anything"

“Okay, okay, it’s not too expensive anyway, 6 euros for a baguette, 2.50 for fries if you want those too for some reason… Brits.Coffee is only 1.50, how much is coffee in England? I bet it is expensive wherever you go? Do you just take your own out?”

“Yeah that’s quite decent actually if it is as good as you’re saying, Coffee from a cafe is almost £3 just for a black coffee, when i was in school you could easily get one for £1.80, absolutely not anymore, the special weird drinks the teenage girls get, sip and throw away are easily £4-5 thou-”

“£5 for a coffee?! What is in it? Cocaine, milk and strawberries? Sorry, bad joke, that’s more than the baguette here, or similar anyway.”

“Yeah it’s very silly, I go to cafes where my friends work frequently so I get the Coffee for free though the food in those cafes…restaurant prices, it is good though, only a treat sometimes you know, I hate paying for food when i’m out however it is a great skill, art and service, you do pay for what you get sometimes, not all the time, you can go to a steakhouse, pay £40-50 and leave disappointed, or £120 if you are on a date, which is why I don’t go on those types of dates, i'm quite stingy really”

“No, I don’t think that stingy, you are just not stupid, you don’t like spending money on things you can get for cheaper, you could make that same steakhouse meal for £10-12 im sure, what was in the whole meal for say, £40? Is that with a drink too? I’m sure that's a ¼ of it at least, no?”

“Really it depends on what steak you get, some of the more expensive cuts are £40 on their own but i usually go for a ribeye, garlic mushrooms as a side and a cocktail or glass of wine, sometimes get a chocolate cake with icecream as a desert, and this is the cheapest steakhouse, if you go to london and go to a fine dining restaurant it’ll be around £80 for the same type of thing, nicer cuts obviously but, yeah I think for that type of meal you could make it yourself for £20 , without the alcohol, but most people have some kind of alcohol in their house and you obviously get more for your money, not a single glass, im guessing it’s quite similar everywhere though, it’s not surprising, more disappointing really. I like going into those types of places high as a kite as I find it funny receiving reactions from the staff as well as other customers, they can’t exactly turn me down, i’ve booked the table, i’m well dressed, but obviously—super high, it’s a feeling of, yep I really am this out of my mind, eating in your fancy establishment, especially on my own

—even when i'm not high, I get similar reactions, I always have a bit of a stoned energy and I think it throws people off, I do like putting people at ease but when they respect me in turn, there's nothing I can do in higher class places to not get judged by people.

“That’s hilarious, I absolutely understand that, i’ve done similar in jobs, though you have to be careful because they can just fire you, fuck most jobs though, waste of time, the money isn’t even worth it and something you love will always come up, one way or another. And yes, Lisbon and Porto are very expensive but that’s mainly due to the tourists.”

“How do you like the music by the way? I’m guessing you are enjoying it from how much you’re tapping, I think I’m gonna sit in the back after we eat if that’s okay, I really need to sleep”

“Yeah we’re not too far off now, I know you didn’t ask me that but…yeah this is great, to be honest I knew it would be, is this the same song? It went from that pretty one into this really relaxing one but I can’t tell if it's just a different part of the same song or if its a different one, I think it's a new one, they just linked them together with a part in the middle didn’t they, i’m already getting the lyrics on this one, very easy listening, I like it a lot, the choruses are predictable and the instrumental bits are far from, its ideal, quite southern sounding but there’s a lot to it”
There’s a good 7 minute silence from discussion as fire on the mountain closes out and fades into not fade away, Guilherme and River pull into Amiens, there's not much parking as it’s quite busy during noon and afternoon period so he parks by the pier, risking a ticket but he hopes to get away with it as he has a fake disability badge he uses in each country, maybe he can convince the parking inspector that there was no space and he desperately needed to eat, maybe he can gain the inspectors sympathy if it comes to it.

“Fucking damn it theres no space, there never is at this time, luckily I have this badge I always use, it works in car parks but we’ll see if this will work, we’ll be quick anyway, I did want us to eat outside though as it’s a nice day, it’s been raining the last 3 days in Saint-Omer.”

“How come you spent so much time in Saint-Omer, there isn't much there unless im mistaken”

“My car had an issue, luckily I found a good mechanic, 50 euros to fix a broken clutch is a great price, I couldn’t do it myself

“Oh right, yeah fair enough”

They get out of the car and head to the Deli Guilherme was raving about.

“Wait I thought we were going to a deli, this looks like a fancy restaurant, are you sure this is the place?

“Deli, restaurant, same thing—We’re just getting the beef-salami-mozzarella baguette and we’ll get coffee from across the river, there's a nice bench facing the river, we can sit there and eat if you like, though you might not want a coffee if you want to sleep after the food, maybe a pastry instead, that’ll make you even more tired, probably”

“Okay yeah, this just doesn’t look like a place that does fancy baguettes for 6 euros, it is so hot though, I will definitely sleep either way and I love coffee.

Guilherme and River walk into the “deli” and Guilherme goes to the counter to order the food while river zones out and looks at the lushious art and plants a designer has perfectly placed around the restaurant in true accordance to the feng shui, River is stunned and takes pictures of every single he can so that he can reference them in his drawings. The food is made quickly as it is mostly pre prepared, they walk out with a large burgundy paper bag with thin cream, cotton ropes delicately threaded through the paper as handles.

“Wow, that’s the nicest takeaway bag i’ve ever seen, the logo even has outer embossing on it, i’ve never seen that, even in London.

“Just wait until you see the baguette, or really, just wait until you try it, the coffee shop is just across the bridge, it shouldn’t be too long of a wait though there is always a bit of a queue in coffee shops no matter where you go, and these guys make a hell of a coffee, or brew, do you guys call it that? Or is that for beer?”

River accidently ignores the question as he's tired and he just says “Okay, it’ll be worth the wait i'm sure, I quite like the wait before food as it makes it better, and then while eating the coffee will cool down to that perfect temperature, what kind of coffee do you drink?

I usually drink an iced americano with 3 shots but i'll just get whatever you recommend"

"Yes I too only drink black coffee, this place doesn't do iced drinks as it's quite traditional, I recommend the extended espresso as it is just perfect, especially if Pablo is working, he's the man."

They reach the coffee shop within a few minutes, like Guilherme promised.

"Pablo! You Italian drug smuggler, it's been a while, what's going on"

"Portugal! You're back again, you can't get enough of France can you?

Pablo calls Guilherme Portugal as he cannot pronounce his name and he has never been able to.

"This freak just came up to me and he wants help getting into spain, I agreed for some reason, i've nothing better to do anyway so yes i'm back again, 2 extended espressos please, I'll take a large cinnamon pastry as well, I can't pronounce it the French way but I always get the same one, you know the one"

"Of course Portugal, it'll be five minutes"

Guilherme goes to take his wallet out of his brown wool shirt pocket; which has a jimi hendrix patch on it, he sewed it on himself and one corner is coming undone slowly.
Pablo winks and puts his hand out “No no” Pablo says in his thick Italian accent, and he winks again at river, “this time is on me, don’t worry

“Enjoy my friend, best coffee you ever have, you will see” Pablo says to River, “And Cinnamon thing, as your new friend call it, no words you will have, straight into siesta after this one yes, just don’t burn in the sun”

River looks at Pablo and then Guilherme, again, grinning from ear to ear. “Thank you so much Pablo, Guilherme spoke some very lovely words about you” “thank you for the coffee, i'm sure i’ll be back when i'm in the area”

“Guilherme is a good man, i’m glad you find him and not some French moustachio hahaha”
He laughs hysterically at his own words and slaps the top of the glass table—making the old ladies jump a little bit, we’re in France however everyone in the restaurant is speaking Italian or Spanish, and intermingling, using both languages, here and there, River’s never seen anything like it and is in that psychedelic type awe you feel when you experience something new, novelty.

River is an absolute blissful hysteria however manages to hold it in, he however cannot stop smiling which draws the attention of the other customers, contagiously making them also smile and wave at him.

After receiving the coffee and the Cinnamon Pastry they make their way to the bench, the one Guilherme was talking about was taken “Damn it that's my favourite one, the other one is blocked by a tree” But as they approach the set of benches, the couple picks up their burgundy takeaway bags, from the same restaurant River and and Guilherme had just bought food from and they carefully drop them into the recycling bin.

“Oh, fortune or luck or whatever, is really on our side today, this is a strange trip, a strange turn of events indeed.”

They sit down on the old wooden bench, well preserved, all original from the 1700s but the lacquer had been redone to seal the colours and grain, a beautiful bench. River commands Guilherme to not sit down so he can take a picture, they then sit down to enjoy their food, they both open their takeaway coffee cups first so they can cool down to that perfect temperature while they eat their prestigious overfilled baguettes.

“Wow, you weren’t joking, these baguettes really are overfilled, this bread is ridiculous, it’s that exact thing you expect, crunchy and crispy on the outside and airy and soft throughout the rest, man what work of art, it’s a shame you eat it and it goes away, I wonder if its just the novelty of the situation or if the baguette really is this nice, can I not get something like this in England?” River laughs to himself, “No, probably not” “This wasn’t 6 euros was it?” River says to his friend. “No no, it was, honestly, look at the receipt, no extra charges either, even if you sit in, great place.”

“You weren’t joking, I really will fall asleep, there’s no way I have room for that pastry, that baguette was a fucking monster, the coffee should be drinkable now”

River goes to sip the extended espresso, and so does Guilherme.

A simultaneous “Mmmmmmmm” and they both laugh hysterically, almost spilling the coffee on their knees in unison, the laugh does not break so they both lean to the ground, one going left and the other going right and they place the coffee cups carefully on the ground as to not spill any”

“Jesus Christ, why is everything so funny and weird?” Guilherme explains.
River still laughing cannot even answer the question so he puts both hands up to signal “I don't know”

River catches his breaths and has a sigh of, not relief, but you know the one. When you’re just content in a moment and you have ultimate presence, and the river is a beautiful teal-zomp colour, with fiery yellow and orange hues reflecting on the surface from the sun, and the reflections of the oak and birch trees dance within the micro details of the ripples.

“Ahh man this is just what I needed, and when you’re present, everything is funny, or beautiful, I guess it’s both man.”

“Yeah it is both, both indeed, they go hand in hand, what a weird thing to have met such a similar person, so weird”

“So weird” River doubles up on Guilhermes statement, a half second later and sighs again as he reaches down to the floor to pick up his coffee”

“It was nice of Pablo to treat us to coffee, is it his shop? I'm sure he has a wife and family to feed, what a lovely gesture, I want to go back to give him money just for being so lovely, it makes you appreciate things so much, maybe i'll give him one of my drawings, it means more than 10 euros, in my opinion, i pour my heart out into these pie-”

“Oh you make art? I didn't know, can I see your drawings?”

“Yeah, of course, let's go back to the car, I really do need to sleep, I think it's been 36 hours at this point, let's use a toilet first, I'm sure you don't like stopping too much”

“No, not really, i'm not in a rush and neither are you, evidently, there's no public restrooms around here, there's one near where we parked on the pier though, I hope the ticket inspector isn't waiting for us, you'll have to fake a disability though, i'm really bad at it, I usually bring a cane or those metal things out but I don't have them anymore.”

“Hahaha, what should I do, limp or pretend to be a retard?”
“Both.” Guilherme says bluntly with a big smile, trying desperately not to laugh”

"Pfff, that'll be fun, why not"

They slowly walk back to the car, River practising his limp and forced retardation, making his new friend laugh hysterically to a point where they can no longer walk and they have to stop to hang onto a handrail.

"This is so so wrong but it is so funny" says Guilherme. "If you can't pretend to be disabled as a joke then I don't want to be alive, it's childish but the context is making it funny, if you were just doing it randomly it would not be funny at all, it's the context."

River stops doing what he was doing and starts walking his normal way again, "Yeah I agree, it's the context that makes it funny, I wouldn't find it funny if you suddenly started walking like a disabled person either, imagine if an actually physically disabled person saw us doing it, that would make me feel bad.

They reach the public restroom at the pier.

20 cents

"Have you got 2 20 cent coins?" River asks, slightly bemused but serious as he desperately needs the toilet, for both purposes.

“I actually don’t” Guilherme says, laughing again at the situation”.

“Oh well” River looks both ways then jumps the spinning metal asterisk barrier.
He laughs as he makes it over and looks back at his friend. “Come on”

“Oh, no I don’t need the toilet, I used the one in the restaurant while you were zoning out; looking at the art, i’ll stop at a petrol station if I need to go”

“Didn’t the coffee do the thing for you?” River asks while slightly hunched and legs shaking, manually.

“Just go you idiot you’re gonna piss yourself” Guilherme says while laughing and pointing behind the river at the graffiti ridden white tiled bathroom “Don’t get stabbed while you’re at it…joking you’re safe” He smiles.

River uses the bathroom and the two of them make their way to the otherside of the pier where the car is parked.

“Oh would you look at that?” Says Guilherme in a confident voice, “No ticket AND no inspector—I’ve done it again.”

They get in the car, Guilherme drives off of the slightly raised curb he had gone up, as he goes through the legitimate car park, they both see the parking inspector, Guilherme, slides the window down with the little plastic rocker, “bon après-midi” He says while waving.
““bon après-midi, au revoir monsieur” The ticket inspector replies with the ticket machine in hand, lowering it to his waist and waving with his pen hand.

He slides the window back up, but not all the way as it is still hot, “Why not?” He says to River, and starts laughing again. “You’re such a maniac” River says to Guilherme. “I mean either way, it’s nice to say hello or good afternoon to people, he doesn’t know that we just parked illegally for an hour, although there still aren’t any free spaces so he might wonder where we came from, maybe we just did a lap of the car park, saw there was no space and left, though we wouldn’t look so happy if that was the case, but no, he won’t think about it at all, great timing though”

“Yeah, great timing, search Dicks Picks .12 on your spotify, that’s a good one, or you like jazz right? If you like 1959, Moanin by Art Blakey is a great one.”

“Ah come on man, i’ve heard that, you’re gonna have to try harder than that”

“Yeah of course that's a classic, uhhh Ahmad Jamal at Pershing, that's 1958 but it’s one of my favourites, so seriously great”

“I’ve heard of him but i'm not sure i’ve listened, is that a good album to sleep to?, is that why you’ve suggested it?”

“I guess my brain does that automatically, I can sleep to anything really but his playing is just stimulating enough to keep my mind from wandering and just quiet enough to relax me.”

“Alright, I’ll give that a go, though you might have to hot spot me, i’m gonna run out of data soon”

“Don’t worry, use my phone, i’ve got it downloaded”

“Perfect, could you show me your drawings before you disappear into dreamland, i'm sure you’ll be out for a while”

“Yeah sure, i’ve got a few sketchbooks with me”

River goes into his bag and gets a sketchbook out and hands it to Guilherme.

“Here you are, they’re mostly not finished but..”

River clears the back seats so he can lay, using his hoodie as a pillow, he lays down while his friend flicks through the sketchbook.

“So which one can I take” Guilherme asks in a cheeky but unserious tone”

“Anyone you want, anyone, I don’t mind, other than the midday sun one, very few of my pieces truly resonate with me and that’s one of them”

“What, really? Any other one? Seriously? Do you not sell them, ill buy one.”

“No, honestly you’ve done so much for me and the trips barely started, you don’t have to pick right away, or I can draw a new one for you, I don’t mind, I make so many I don’t even think twice about giving them to people, especially people I like, it’s an act of love and service for me, that’s the way I see it.”

“Wow thank you, I love art but i I don’t own much, it’s quite expensive, do you make much from these”

“Uhh not really, £20-30 a piece, when they do sell, but they don’t really, and i don’t mind, people have to spend money on food and rent and everything essential, which is why I like giving them to people, I like the love I receive back through words and expressions, that’s a form of payment in itself, even the ones I don’t give to people, the feedback I receive is wonderful, even if I don’t resonate with the piece, which is quite strange, I make them yet I don’t resonate with them most of the time, like when musicians make a hit song or album and in the interview they call it garbage or “ohhh that was a bad song I can’t believe that did well” I never used to understand that but I do now.”

“Yeah I kind of get that, well this sun is beautiful, I’ll take this one, I’ll put it on my dashboard for when it’s rainy.”

“Thats beautiful, I’ll carefully tear it out for you when I wake up”

“Have a good rest, we’ll be close to the Spanish border when you wake up though i’ll probably need to sleep by then, i’m sure you won’t mind drawing in that time, I can give you the key so you can go outside but make sure you lock the door I don’t want any truck stop gipsies breaking in”

River laughs “Don't worry, I’m okay staying in the car, though I’ll need to pee again, I probably won’t sleep for that long, I never do in cars, though I do love sleeping in cars, I love the vibration."

River quickly falls asleep to the second song in the album.

"Wow what a weird dream" River says upon waking, Guilherme is still driving, "How long did I sleep for, it's still day"
"Only about two hours, you okay? What was the dream?"
I was walking down a very familiar road and almost got hit by a truck, though I was sure that I was on the pavement, and there was a poetic monologue going the whole time, let me write it down and i'll read it to you, it was about ignorance and society, I wonder what my subconscious was trying to tell me, so odd, give me a second"
"Do you write poetry as well? Or was that a one off? Maybe you could combine the poetry with the ink drawings you do, I think it would be too much with the painted or coloured ones, though I shouldn't give you advice i'm not an artist, though some of your pieces already do have words on them, very abstract though, I like it, the viewers gets their own meaning, is that the point? "*I've been lost for so long I may never find my way back, oh well*"

It's interesting, I remember that one and I only saw it once, maybe you should write more, you'll have a lot of time on this trip, that's for sure."

"I write but I wouldn't call it poetry it's more...trying to land somewhere in a world of symbols, lost meanings, confusion, love but also anger and hate, i'm not sure what i'm trying to say or do in life, which is why I like getting lost in the arts, not that I think i'll find some kind of meaning however as I don't think there is inherent meaning to the world, we create it and maybe to our detriment as it creates some form of expectation. Even the way we set a goal or target, as if we think it is the correct one, did Jesus have a goal or was he just living his truth, living ultimately for the sake of living, I feel as though we are self writing puppets in a way, I believe or think that there is free will in some form or another but not the way "most people" see it, I feel as though it is like a pilot in an aeroplane making micro adjustments so that it stays on course, second to second control of reality takes utmost presence, but it always drops no matter what, I don't believe anyone can completely present, and completely in control, all the time, I think you have to let reality...

...the universe, God; do its own thing as it knows what it's doing, it seems when we try to take control of the universe, nature, God; that things go wrong, the flow of the universe, or the natural order of things, the Tao, has a mind of it's own and I guess really, it doesn't matter all too much, like the Taxi driver that drove me to Dover said "Whats going on down here will go on either way, you needn't worry about it"

"So yes then, you do write poetry, you seem to be trying to be everything at once, that must be an interesting way of living, if not tiring"

"Man I wish i was tired, it's me trying to feel like i've accomplished anything at all which even gives me this thought im trying to write right now, or the fact I am on this journey with you now, what i'm trying to say is, I want to be tired but I never do feel like I am, or in the right way, there was maybe 2-3 months, I really felt that way, like I could relax, my shoulders drop back as if they deserved to be, i would be asleep by 11pm, i'd wake up at 4am for what I used to call my 2nd evening, then would wake up again at 8am to start my day and go into university, it was when I lost that flow of life where I lost touch with myself really, on a deep level, I understand and have always understood you can't always be in the same flow however I very much grew attached to it, dare I say i loved it even, the routine of it, it was also the most strong my relationship to my girlfriend at the time was"

“But yes, I guess it is tiring, maybe I should just focus on the elements I love most, jazz, poetry and drawing, it’s almost like I'm not even listening to myself anymore, almost as if I don’t trust myself but if I cannot trust myself then who can I trust? A stranger to drive me around europe? An imaginary God I don’t really believe in or the whimsical who knows what of the free universe, I like that one the best though really, even the mantras and meditations only go a certain way. It really is about the relationships as without those am I really? I only know myself through my family and friends, how they see me and how I see them informs me on who I am, truly”

“Well you’ll be happy to know we’re only 3 and a half hours away from the border, that album was great, what should we listen to next? Shall I put something on? You know America, self-titled? 73 is i-”

“72, but yes, it’s one of my favourite albums man, i’ve never even driven to it, that should be illegal man.”

“Yes, and I am the one arresting you for that offence, that is an illegal action, have you got your passport by the way? I’m guessing so since you got to France from England?”

“Yeah I do, though I was smuggled across the border—to save money of course, I have 220 euros still, from when I left over, I’ve not even spent a penny, maybe I didn’t even need it though I couldn’t risk leaving with—-nothing, you know, though i’m paying for the next meal and that’s not up for debate, i'll tie you up if need be, no wait that sounds very wrong, does that kind of humour make sense in your language and culture?”

“Uhh yeah I guess so, we like a bit of kinky gay humour in Portugal though if I was French I’d think that you were taking the piss out of me, that's a saying I learned in England the one I was there, it’s a good one though how do you take the piss OUT of someone. Of course you were smuggled, you smell like someone that could have been smuggled, was it scary being in the bit underneath? I did it once but on a short boat trip, not good really, so much risk, though you reach the other side and you feel like you’ve gotten away with murder, God, I know a lot of sayings, I might as well be British eh? Bruv.”

“Yeah im starting to think you’re putting the accent on honestly, you’re tripping me the fuck out.”
“Now I've never heard that one, what does that mean? Trip like drugs or?”

"Yeaaah I guess like drugs, yeah, psychedelics create what in hippie lingo we call a trip, similar to this but usually stationary as it's so profound you don't really want to move, though when you do walk, bike or i'm guessing drive or be driven on a psychedelic it's a whole new animal, it's as if the stagnant thoughts blow away with the wind and the crust of your skin regenerates and creates a new level and you can feel it in real time"

"Yes yes, no I have taken psychedelics before, I get it, I made the mistake of driving on LSD once, I won't go into that however—Shall we pull over at this petrol station"

"It's called 'Don't Stop', maybe we should listen and wait for another one, maybe we're better off dead, than stopping at that one, eh?"

"What does that even mean, no let's stop, we have to now, what cool hedges around it, you can take pictures of every angle like you always do, weirdo"

"Yeah why not maybe it will make a cool album cover one day, though i'm not sure what kind of music will go with the name Don't Stop, I'm not sure what that means I thought it rolled off my tongue quite nicely though—

‘Don’t Stop, you’re better off dead’ Maybe i'll talk to the owner and suggest that as the name, though it wont make for a good sign, I guess it makes you want to stop though if it’s telling you not too, red button and all that”

River and Guilherme park right out front and head into the petrol station.

“Key rings, do you want one, so you can show all your family and friends that you’ve been to a random petrol station just 15 miles north of Spain, and you’ve bought a Eiffel tower keyring? You can say you went to the Eiffel tower, how cool!” In an ironic dry tone, he obviously picked up from Brits or, TV, or something—who knows with this guy”

“Hahaaa, yeah for sure, i’ll buy 3 or 6, what’s the deal?” River says enthusiastically to the guy at the counter.

Okay man let’s keep driving, we’ve taken up enough time, you got your keyrings right, though you’ll probably lose them, what a waste of of 12 euros, oh well, the badly cast metal will a certain impression with you in some regard, sometimes it’s more about the purchase than the the purchase itself, weirdly enough, like a vintage garment you know won’t fit very well but you were at a certain market at a certain time with a kind of slim budget and you caught just the right item.

yeah let's go, it's getting late, god the petrol is steep here maybe we should have waited but I was running low, maybe I should mount one of those eiffel towers as a hood ornament as a joke, though it'll get stolen, paint my car in the french colours while i'm at it, that'll be funny won't it."

"I'm not too sure, maybe let's do a Polish eagle to throw people off, NOW that will be funny if anything."

"We're close to Spain now, and I mean it, really close. I think we should stop in a motel or hotel when we get there, rather than sleeping in the car again, which might be nice.

They approach the Spain sign and Guilherme starts singing very loudly but in a purposefully funny accent.
Where's the nearest motel? River asks, though I really don't mind sleeping in the car again.
No no we'll find a motel, we can share a room with 2 beds, unless you're gay.
Hah, that's fine man.

The two of them check in to a hotel, not motel, I guess Guilherme had the money so why not, River apprehensively agreed as he wanted sleep, if he wasn't in a cycle of smoking cannabis or doing other psychoactive compounds, he loved his sleep, even with the former he did but, getting out of that cycle every now and again helped him rest and reset, change his point of view on everything, functional drug abuse goes a certain way for a creative but it's due to the contrast with so called sobriety, I say so called because in today's climate it is seen as the best thing, people congratulate each other on their abstinence from... whatever it may be they're using, yet people also hold a spitefulness against it not so secretly, oh you're sober now, no, I am just not drinking, I am just not smoking or snorting, I am not sober, and it's a boring word. People love labels, you're either a determinist or you believe in free will. You state one view and you're a postmodernist, I write yet I am not a writer. In some cases labels or names are useful, functional. Recently I've noticed people like to dispel mental health labelling, in this particular case it is useful, not in terms of diagnosing really however, it's grouping symptoms together, if there is an effective treatment you can find it a whole lot easier, if you are generally anxious, you know what you can work on, similar to getting any other medical diagnosis, depression often leads to serious physical illnesses, though it starts in the mind it does spread, I've felt it myself, a true... Brain flu.

I have to admit however I believe too much attention is placed on the so-called illness itself and not what you can do about it, actively. It may be called an illness or disorder yet everyone's disorder is specific to them in some way, it's how THEIR brain functions and processes information.

It's a pretty nice hotel actually, shame it's just one night, balcony with a nice view, they didn't see the night before, basement level spa, included in the price too and a breakfast of course, I think Guilherme paid extra and didn't tell me.

I love interesting people, or characters as I call them, which I don't think people understand what I mean when I say, I see life as a grand play, some people are characters and some people are just not and it's fine either way, some fit straight into archetypes and some make you question the idea of archetypes entirely, is he a jester or is he just a crackhead? You may never find out if you don't inquire, I like inquiring, it's fulfilling seeing everything and everyone the world has pumped out, "how did you understand what he just said, I didn't catch a word" Well, I'm fluent in crackhead. It might sound like I favour characters but I've learned a lot from squares too, for example, how to not be a square.

Squares are a functional building block of functional, interior society, some should do it, but not me, I can shapeshift into a square at will but it has wobbly edges and a true rectangle can see those wobbles, and try to iron them out, keyword there is try, I've never fit into any rectangular role, I wobble too well for my own good but it's how I like to walk, 4 inches off the ground and leaning left. I'm not sure on the purpose of these observations yet they just keep on coming, it's fun to observe and analyse the observation, but not too deeply, it makes me ill diving, too deep but also not surface level, the Tao in function through observation.
You can't ask for much if you don't also give and selling doesn't count, that's for sure.
I find it interesting, hearing someone's whole story and months later you notice it doesn't pan out the way they wanted, but they play it off as if it were, that's life really, carrying on, I do want to know though, was it a toxic relationship or not, I really do love observing don't I.

What time did you get up? You don't strike me as an early bird. Guilherme says, wiping his eyes and moustache.

Around 8 I think, Guilherme, have you ever noticed that apples taste sweeter when you bite into them then leave them for a few minutes before biting them again? People usually don't like when apples brown but I think it's just in their minds.

Wait what, it's too early for that, you just don't stop, do you. I don't think I've ever thought about the change in an apple's taste after a bite, it's just an apple. I would have hated to be your dad when you were a kid, a lot of I don't know answers.

Yeah you're right, I'll shut up. I say, closing my book.

Oh no no, carry on, it's interesting, it looks like you've written a lot today, what else came to mind?

Do you see a separation in humans, characters and non characters? Or to word it better, free souls and people trapped in a box? Of their own definitions, or worse yet, someone else's.

Jes.. Uhh yeah I think I know what you are getting at with that one, I've met a lot of both types, the characters tend to be more interesting right? One question, am I a character or a box human?

You were singing nonsensical Spanish songs while going across the border and you own one t-shirt, you are a character.

Okay, good. What else is in your book? I see more.

Oh nothing, I was pondering on mental illness and the need for labels, it's too tricky to really... FiFind an answer to what I was asking but I'll keep asking, I think it's just my personal opinion actually. I've noticed that people tend to stick to their labels quite strongly, as if their lives depend on it, rather than using, say, a grouped set of symptoms as a way of planning what they need to work on. People love using the, I'm ADHD, thing as a kind of personality trait but I think it's quite disrespectful to those with the actual disorder, which isn't to say a said person has not got an attention deficit but for most it's something we can work on, I can't focus yet I'm 90 pages to a book, how did that happen? Some things are measurable, scanning brain waves, it doesn't take a psychologist or psychiatrist to see a depressed person, they almost smell depressed, you can hear a sad piano coming from one's soul, the sulk in the shoulders of a businessman not meeting his quote for the third quarter, he's in debt and his children hate him, his wife's cheating on him...

...he knows yet he wants the illusion of keeping his family together, even though it's more damaging, that to me anyway is depression, you can find homeless people that are not depressed, they may not be the happiest, but they also might.

I thought it was nothing, that's something, they say ADHD cones from trauma, and new age people say you can fully heal from trauma so... No ADHD? If you really don't want to have it, the hyperactivity part seems like having a lack of places to channel your energy I see you tapping like a mad man when you haven't drummed or drawn or written for a while, I think for some of us it's natural for our brains to stray, I think it's why ADHD folks love video games, a fun thing maybe, but imagine that level of concentration and time put into... art? New skills? Kind of like what you do, some people just seem to have an infinite bank of energy, others less, and I guess it's cool? Some jobs or practices really don't take that much energy, not necessarily easy but, you play at your level you know, debating stupid people doesn't make you smarter, only dumber.

“Where has culture gone and who took it away? How is ‘everyone’ dressed’? as if they’re walking through a car-boot sale in Turvey yet I love car-boot sales, what is going on, what are you talking about, your kids going camping? “Were the tents already there then?” Why on this fucking conky ass earth would the tents already be there, what? Just say anything, make sure someone hears it.

“We always have a great breakfast buffet when we go to Milton Keynes…went to waga’s though this time” I’ve no commentary to add to that one. Where is the fucking toilet in this place, 1 establishment split into 2, with a staircase going to flats in the middle, wheres the toilet, you’re selling food, coffee and bubble-bullshit-tea-beef-bulgogi it was okay, came out too fast, I wish it was grilled or fried on spot, it was nice, eh.

I appreciate the happiness and joyousness of children and what they bring to the world but I don’t remember acting that way or being loud for loudness sake, and I have confirmed with my parents that I was in fact not that way.

I'd annoy myself if i was making constant noise, even the sound of my laptop keyboard annoys me and i try typing quieter to not hear it as much but then I slow my flow-down and I think at the pace of a coke-head on meth, coming down from LSD, craving a cigarette and a…well nothing.

Walking around a city i've been to a few times, without a phone, you notice a lot yet it slips away, the menial-utter-boringness of a city life, when I see people having genuine fun I smile and laugh, they don't need to see that i'm smiling, it's not a relatable thing like someone on a train sighing after every stop, making clicking noises with their mouths, haha yeah long train isn't it yeah, long one this one, it's a shame you chose to be here in this moment; making a noise to affirm that you are alive, sniffling every 35 seconds on repeat with one additional half sniffle in between and a well rounded sniff when it hits the one minute mark, at least he got off 3 towns-not-even-stops before Bedford, nice."

From a trip to Cambridge, River says, looking at Guilherme inquisitively.

Did you not have headphones or something? Why were you so angry, he laughs and lights a cigarette, takes a massive drag.

I thought you didn't smoke?! And you can't smoke in these rooms but I'm gonna join you.

It's too early for a joint and I haven't even got any, I want something in my lungs.

Yeah, yeah, shall we find some weed?

Yeah, easy. You know River, I had a crazy thing happen to me last night.

Ooooh, what was it? I love it already.

A kind of.. Spirit?... Angel? Came to visit me, it didn't feel like a dream, I could see the ceiling, and the mirror, that weirdly over painted red door, there's like 4 layers on that thing, it barely closes, anyway, she was beautiful, a floating soul with flowing hair, and I say it felt like it wasn't a dream, it felt like she was leading me through a dream, more like the catalyst of a lucid hallucination.

Oh, what did she say? She did not say anything other than “when you see the girl with the golden hair.. “ but it wasn't the speech that was significant, it was the way she led me through this experience, showing me open doors on this infinitely wide wall, when we stepped out of the door there was an impossibly steep and tall hill, with one cow at the top, a windows xp type blue sky, you know the one the hill was, startlingly green, almost too bright to look at.

Wow, what an experience, she said nothing else?

It's strange because I feel like I've seen her before somewhere, I don't believe in such things but I feel like she opened up a portal for me, the first time I saw her I left my job that morning, this is the 2nd time I've seen her and... well I'm confused what she meant, am I experiencing nostalgia because my first girlfriend had ginger hair or? From a Jungian perspective she was more a mother figure than a lover or... Whatever the word is.

Funnily enough I wrote a piece on nostalgia yesterday, I remembered what a friend had told me and it inspired me.

"Post nostalgia, a term I've not heard or coined before, a nostalgia for the present and the present future rather than a past memory, it'll break you to keep dragging your feet, someone or something will lift you, someone will hold you, happy sad is the best happy, the best sad, no words come to mind when I think of her as she always beats me to it, as it won't leave my lips"

Post nostalgia, what an interesting term, I've never heard it either, it sounds like a drop off from the positivity of the feeling of nostalgia however you've worded it so gracefully, as a positive thing, pondering on a memory and letting it go, allowing for the new to come in, a balance between nostalgia and novelty. Anyway we can continue talking in the car, they're gonna kick us out soon, better leave before they realise that we smoked in the room.

They skip on the breakfast that Guilherme obviously paid for, oddly enough.

I think Siyuan was right about intention actually, it's a precursor to action, it's hard to act without intent, I still don't like the way she said it though. Even if you're improvising, the intention is... Improvising? Or just being present to allow improvisation?

Who's Siyuan?

Oh I thought I mentioned her earlier, the Chinese girl, seaweed, some of my friends called her, not to her face.

Right yeah, Singapore woman.

Don't you think culture is weird? I said very abruptly, is it dying or would you still call it culture? Some is obviously "intact" but it may be too subjective to fully create a objective opinion or stance on anyway, take the evolution of the culture in the UK for example, it used to be viewed as a kind of prestige or a high end living, the royal family and castles etc, how did it evolve to be such a street based-youthful culture? Did the youth always dictate the flow of culture?

My girl goes home today

My girl goes home today and i'm stuck in a house, bricks and mortar yet nothing keeps it up. 10:54, oh fuck i've missed it already, I might as well go to bed. Here's the new employee rushing through the woods to the new job he's bound to start, resentful but full of heart, spinning green, morphine-esc nose infusion reminiscing of a quiet wilderness in mind, a kind only a peaceful childlike mind can provide, nothing I can use to land, no sobriety I can see in the future for me and it has nothing to do with belief, i'm too much a creep, i'll have to keep moving until my sunken feet begin to seize, maybe I should I learn to drive, nothing has anything to do with belief, maybe i'll stop by the trees, i'm late for work and i've arrived at the holiday camp, 13:04, i've already missed my first shift, or training, what are they training me for just throw me straight in— I cant do it anyway and the man training knows, "Thanks for not falling asleep" yes but maybe next time I will if you don't speed it up.

The camp is beautiful though it's filled with the right type of trees, if you know what I mean, the type that nature wants to sprout, not the 'Controlled deforestations, don't worry, we're only removing trees due to overgrowth, this will allow space' yes, like social distancing in nature, how very nice, dead trees; no bees, but let's not be negative it is a beautiful space, it's a shame I have to work.

The key seems to work and it's not an electric one, I like that, a real key, those electric thob's don't feel like i'm entering a permanent destination but a hotel, I know there is no permanence to anything but at nicely casted key on a satisfyingly round keychain with Fidel Castro looking at me, "who's the dude", Fidel Castro but i've no clue what he did, i'm gonna get Hitler and Stalin next for just this exact convo, though it may be bad karma, though it doesn't work that way, little do many people know.

A zoom rings out at 13:30 to all the folks who missed the morning meeting.Rob, an Italian gentleman I'm yet to meet, is already drunk, and starts talking first before the manager even says, "What meeting, I thought we were starting tomorrow".
"Well, no one has turned up so I guess we shall start tomorrow and this will be the first briefing"

2 people drop from the call Bobby and Cherry, Jesus what a bad name, maybe when I meet her it'll make sense, maybe she goes by Cher as well, Christ, even worse; never mind.

There are 3 of left on the line other than the manager, we're all supposed to be line cooks and bar staff, general camp moderators, maybe i'll try for that one, standing around making sure everything is in order "yep, yep, that's all good, yeah let's move that bench there to keep the flow smooth, I know what i'm doing, I have got a lanyard after all, with a laminated badge, 'camp moderator'" Yep that's me, mr camp moderator. "Okay, well let's do the meeting tomorrow then since there's been a mishap in communication." Yeah let's call it a mishap, anyway.

Next door is a pretty, kind of short, little bit too skinny, girl called Malina, maybe i'll try getting her attention by sitting on this lovely wooden chair out the back of huts and say nothing, make sure she sees my Bob Dylan t shirt and my moderately sized joint twirling in my hand but not lighting it for a while as the tunes play to show self control, it can't be Dylan song that'd be too movie like and she wouldn't get it anyway, Blaze Foley perhaps, no that's also too much.

Eyes of the world by the Grateful Dead, perfectly musical, beautiful lyrics that will maybe get her attention, as I don't know what to say to such a pretty thing, i'll let the lyrics speak for me, for some reason girls have always come to me and i've never had to do the first step but maybe that's why I always attract the wrong ones, I always think I should say something first but I never do, and it seems wrong, I have no intention really, i'm just here and perhaps that's just it, i'm looking for other people that are just "here" no purpose, no reason or cause. One of the first things one of my previous partners asked was "What's your intention" in quite an aggressive manner, I was caught off guard and simply said, "I have no intention". "Intention is important, intention is everything, again what is your intention"Like a Chinese police guard rather than exchange student, Maybe I was in the wrong but I have no answer to a question like that, maybe it is my 'spiritual' standing or just the way I was brought up but to have intention to me is to be looking for something, and especially when it comes to a person, i'm not looking for anything but them, I said my girl goes home today; it's a, not a metaphor but a kind of feeling for the future.

Malina is on the out back porch while the song hits 7:37, good timing as the delicious jam has just kicked in and I've paid no attention, I think they like that but with a kind of slight side eye to show you have acknowledged them. Vegan birkenstocks, tapping on the off-beat with her left foot, down beat on the right that's odd, great size too, size 5? Not in a sexual way, but also in a sexual way, can't get around that it's human nature, well mine. Flowing floral skirt with an unnecessary additional off-white coloured belt high on her waist—no band tee, thank God, whatever it would be, I know I wouldn't like it, nor a lousy throw over blouse due to nothing else to wear, not that I care, it looks like she's made the jumper, or someone else has, but it fits perfectly with the skirt so she must have, inverse colour way of the skirt and the patterns slightly different, she's made it for that exact outfit, outrageous, she's tried matching it but not exactly, not too be cheesy, I get it, I get it.

"Hey, you're working as a camp coordinator too right?" She says lightly, leaning on her side on the chair, I guess expecting a longer conversation.
"Yeah yeah, I mean it was one of three positions but good guess, you too? I guess it worked, she spoke first, how would you not? I'm basically wearing a dress too and what guy wears a dress, well more a hindu tunic, also in birkenstocks.

maybe we can talk about how the environment is going to shit and we can both save it with our vegan birks and homemade clothes, though the tunic is from Zara, it was on sale I had to, i'll take the tag off and pretend it's from India, no, she's a girl she'll know.

"Yeah, yeah me too, glad I got that one. I'm good at cooking but I'm not too sure about Americans and...kids, I feel like I can just dance around and help out when needed with this one, enjoy the sun, what camp are you in? Jefferson? I guess so if you're housed here, it's so cheesy that they've named them after presidents but, I guess that's America for you"

"Yeaaah, Americans, right? Yeah I'm working in the same camp, where are you from? That's a sweet accent you've got" I asked quite cheekily and complimentary.

"A little Island off of Spain but I've lived all over Spain, I love it but I need a change, everything becomes the same after a while and you need something new you know, I guess you're the same, you're British? But based on your face you're not originally British?"

"Yeah I thought America would be a nice change, new environment, new people, help out a little bit...yeah I don't really know where i'm from so i'll keep it at that."

"Hmmm mysterious, I like that, you could be from anywhere though, and the British accent kind of centres it in a nice way, that's very cool, i'd guess Turkish but you're not hairy enough, no offence, if that is offensive, I know men are more sensitive than women" She laughs, delightfully.

"Why don't you bring your chair over, since we're talking already"

The view is beautiful and the sun is at its peak, the lake is in the distance and the sea a little further, just out of view but still in view, if you know what I mean, you can see the tops of the white sails, and the trails of the large ferries and cargo ships, the pine are like I said, the perfect kind, just dense enough for you to feel cuddled by nature and as if you're in a forest but sparse enough that you can look through it, to an extent.

"Yeah why not, shall I make tea? What are you drinking" Malina asks as she stands up almost instantly, with that kind of twirl where you are unsure if she knows what she's doing to a man's mind, I'm sure she knows.

"I'm drinking green tea with lemon and mountain honey, i've got plenty but if you'd prefer something else, bring it over, we can mix and match, though that might be weird, i'm quite specific about my flavours"

“Hah you’re weird, no, green tea is fine, I love mountain honey, you can barely call the plastic squeezy kind honey, I’ll just be a second; I don’t know why I wore a jumper, it goes with my outfit so I thought i’d brave the heat until sunset but…it’s probably 28 degrees”
Malina gets changed into a white band t shirt but it seems to be an obscure Spanish band, or something, who knows actually it could be her favourite cafe”

“These rooms are great huh? Just spacious enough for everything, kitchen for cooking, bathrooms never have to be big, it's a waste of space.”
“Yeah I agree”
I pull my chair to the right of the patio, ruining my view with the wooden pillar, making space for her to pull her chair up, they were nice chairs though hardwood so we both had the same idea of softening the blow with the cushions provided, probably better to sit on the patio floor with blankets but maybe leave that for later, if we feel that way.

“Hey are you gonna light that joint, or are you just gonna twirl it like some kind of fake prophetic poet—Dylan after all, come on, talk about a cliche hippy? And a fake hindu dress? Fair enough, you had to get it, i’m the same, the environments on pause when somethings on sale, someone else will buy it”

“Hah, yeah I was gonna wait for the peak of the song actually but i’ve already missed it”
*twirls joint one time, looks Malina in the eyes, then lights the joint, spinning it to ignite all sides, it is a 0.5 afterall, I dont actually know but i’ve always called that size of joint a 0.5, probably more a 0.7 from how quickly I go through a 3.5 gram bag, (remember the old adidas three stripe 7g bags though), I always knew my favorite guy, A1, first letter, first number on the keyboard, first on the contact list, smart guy, was giving me too much and he didn’t mind sitting with me for an hour or talking about the state of Luton or how hot the area had become, I remember one time; We met by the corner shop on Elizabeth street, off of Farley hill, police pulled up at the same time, I kept sat on the bench-having acknowledged him and the police, he got out of his car looked at me and went straight in the shop, meanwhile another guy buying something ran straight at him, same wave length “I had to throw them of G, there onto the new whip n that” he said in his funny North London accent, “Yeah nah I know man that’s why I sat still, that guy just ran at you though what the fuck man”, “Yeah, nitty cuz, did you see his face”

He even backed me from a far once when one of his boys said “he's weird man”, “nah he's cool leave him”

“Interesting story, thank you for that one, it’s nice to know you buy from people you like rather than just anyone…”

“Yeah I mean it changes the entire experience, it’s the vibrations it transmits, as silly as that sounds i know..”

“No no I get it, buy from someone you don’t like and you’re unlikely to enjoy the cannabis, though I'm not sure it’s the same with food? Interesting one huh? Maybe it’s a happy coincidence? Good guy, good weed? Or well, it’s not a coincidence really, maybe the worst types of dealers just have the worst weed, it kind of makes sense

Malina is a one of a kind human, you couldn't write her up if you tried, where’d you find that one, and that one too, close her down and she has one for you in return just like that, she can't be stopped just because she couldn’t be, not for the sake of it, like people acting weird for no reason, you’re not weird you’re trying to be, someone is either cute or not, to me or any other single human, probably.

The can't sleep rhapsody with too eyes closed but the third one wide open, maybe it's the way it should be and maybe I just get annoyed for no reason over things I cannot control, but the fact I cannot just feel the way that I want to feel annoys me, a full day of doing energy heavy—things, and I still don't feel like sleeping, I don't even feel like writing yet, here I am writing, for what reason? To sell a book? No, probably not...If i can take anything from making art for the last 8-10 years is that it's extremely hard to sell yet we keep at it for no reason at all rather than to do it, which is absolutely insane, I see other creatives manage to turn off—go for a drink, smoke a cigarette, have a laugh—even at a festival I can't sit still, if i'm not the one on stage playing drums and i'm not enjoying the music then it's a "why am I not performing right now with my band, we're better than they're and i'm sure this crowd would like to hear the same setlist 3 times today, we're basically the new led zeppelin crossed with 3 jazz bands and Neal Cassady as the conductor, who wouldn't love us." The problem is no one knows Led Zeppelin anymore, or the three jazz bands, take your pick, it could be any, and maybe one other person in the whole of England knows who Neal was, a fucking cowboy, let's get that much straight.

I'm trying to change and still I won't, the cannabis has left me, even the cigarettes, these nicotine pouches don't even feel like nicotine in the same capacity so I barely count it, they seem to mellow out a social space quite nice or something like that, a slight something when I'm writing but that's about it. 11mg down to 6 down to 3 to 1.5, hey no, maybe perhaps I like these, back up the ladder, 11mg today, sometimes 2, I'll write until I have a headache and physically cannot keep writing, I've drawn and written with a pen so much today I had no choice but to go back to the keys, keyboard, okay laptop. The wine's in the cellar, I don't know just quite where—I don't really want any anyway, it just sounds like a blues, where it could it be if anywhere, it's there in your mind, you're a criminal yet you're walking a tight line, we don't feel so sublime like the octopus from the dead sea and the Macedonian fine wine, it was okay at best I won't lie—How could she drink so much if one glass made her that sloppy, it was only 9%, or something like that I can't really remember, nor why should i it's useless information, that word should be info-mation, honestly, and a southern American accent saying it only, either black or white I don't mind, an Asian Kentuckian? My all means man, fire away.

River and Malina walk up to the camp management thing, office, yeah, discarding a joint nearing it, we'll come back for that there was quite a lot left, we both said, no laughter on that one, it was the honest—sincere truth, and I think we needed one for the briefing we're about to have.

"Since none of you decided to sho–"

Yeah yeah we get it, I won't do the entire transcript but something on the lines of powerpoint presentation A-Z, 1 through 9, just over there where you can't see it, yeah rightly so. I'm sick of this let's just stand around on a camp all day instructing down syndrome folks how to swim, or whichever cult it was I can't remember, I wasn't listening, we start tomorrow, good thing they briefed us today and not yesterday then, I don't even smoke any more and I want a joint or a cigarette, strictly no drugs policy at the camp as it is Christian, I mean the cannabis doesn't count it's strictly medical and I need it get by, bipolar, autistic spectrum disorder, OCD, traits of a celebrated vet yet no medals nor a discharge, not of that kind anyway, no, none of that kind either i'm very clean.

We got a tour of the entire camp and then another one, of the bit we'd be patrolling, making sure the little rats didn't drown or hang themselves from being bored of being at a shitty holiday camp there parents sent them to, to keep them away for an entire month, pretty good, I'd probably do the same if I hated my kids, it was probably just me but I always hated 'planned activities', something 'days', which is why when I see the word workshop in my mid 20s it makes my skin crawl, utterly, severely, more so than 7 Nytol, quite an itchy substance that one, not more than morphine though, or oxycodone as it's the closest i've come, though the first time I bought ketamine the guy didn't know what it was, "oh no yeah my guys got some" who knows what that was but I couldn't move, I didn't pass out or die either but it was somewhere in between, funnily enough poppy derivative drugs are listed as a stimulant, I guess for crackheads like me they are, though they also make me sleep, multiple strains? Like weed? Huh, maybe I should tell the ones in town to get the other kind as they could do with some motion in their legs, I mean I can't walk straight, but they should, if they want to, there's that one dude in a mobilised scooter thing, he might as well have a TV on the front of it with a mug and ashtray attachment on the side, I don't think it even works, or he just never moves from that spot.

But I think i'm probably done with ketamine anyway, unless someone else has some, it doesn't really do that much really when you think about it, maybe the occasional use to fully disintegrate all my already separate parts, but no I actually think I like it, too much, I know myself well and I just kept snorting until i physically couldn't do anymore, or rather I had enough and I started getting lifted from my bed and spinning 360 and a pharaoh came through my ceiling and showed me how to draw straight lines without a ruler, I'll keep my phone charging over night though it's no use to me anyway, downing a strongbow is completely fine though yeah, and 1200mg of gabapentin, absolutely fine, I should probably stop doing that too but I can't sleep without cannabis and it's frustrating getting almost a nights worth of sleep every 3 days, I've always had insomnia but it feels like an excuse at this point because at a young age it would just be a few hours and some night terrors and now it's all night or almost, the entire thing, i'm tempted to just go back to smoking cannabis, i'm probably doing more damage taking random chemicals in random intervals, 3 joints a day was fitting, when I was in a beautiful routine with it, I had something to look forward to, something that made life worth living, that might sound like a pessimistic take but it's actually a rather hopeful one as I can't see an alternative and I do infact want to be alive.

I love this incarnation though it's come with a few faults, though I cant shame myself nor anyone else for those, birth defects, defects gathered along the way.

Forgetting where I am while on a bike ride, how did i get here, a phone call telling me that the concert is coming close, yeah your gonna miss it you can bike or i'll give you lift, no no I have too pride ill bike and fall over and scrape the same wrist I have 3 times, I can't believe I blacked out, that was the first time in my life and it really looked like people were having a good time. "Yeah maybe you should stick to the weed or a beer or two" Malina says caringly and sweetly, but if you can limit it to that, i'm sure they all care and don't want to see you that way, what made you even go in such a state, I would have just stayed home and laid in bed, either way, at least you turned out safe"

It turns out it's an all encompassing camp, Christian, down syndrome and kids, well no just down syndrome folks but they stand out you know, and they're the happiest of the kind though a little bit dribbly, happy to see you once they know you like a dog when you come home, though they can talk, you can't really make out what they say but hey at least they're trying to you know. How can you even write a book when you've experienced nothing of life?

I guess it happens on its own. I remember thinking quite "profoundly" about life when I was about 5 but I never knew what to channel it into. What did you do with your youth? Malina?

Uhhh, I guess I was quite the same, I never did homework because I knew it would end up the same, or thought it would, maybe I would be at Oxford studying a fake medicine or something though who knows, I always enjoyed just making a mess, for messes sake you know, see what happens, get some old clothes, stitch a few shitty lines, throw some paint on it "oh that looks nice" yeah I like it, I mean it's shit but it's my shit, I never quite knew what I wanted, ever, even now, looking at you it makes me a bit more confident that I am in fact on the right track, I mean look at you, it's as if I drew you and then dipped the drawing into LSD and then tripped on Mescaline and manifested you into reality, i'm not quite sure what i'm looking at, yet, the more I look at it, the more I like it, yes, this is my kind of flirting, just being absolutely straight forward, though I would like for you to have longer hair but we can work on that by just waiting and i'm sure you feel the same way, being a; rocker? Jazzer? Poet and musician, like what are you? I didn't mention the weed because parents don't like weed even though they know the good that it does for us, you'd have to do every drug under the moon for them to see how beneficial cannabis really is.

not that it's an excuse but i feel like we can recognise what it does for us, is it just me or...well I can relax without it but it's not a real relaxation, it's a what if kind of relaxation, again i'm sure we're all different but we're listening to Bob Dylan right now with a massive joint of Blue Dream mixed with Northern lights. It's not like beer or MDMA, or anything else, benzos, god forsake them, everything is temporary, even Cannabis, but it almost just does something more, it leave a little lasting something or another, an idea or a spiritual something, do you not just smoke a hit of a joint after a while and have the aahhhhhh fucking hell that's just what I needed, maybe an alcoholic, or someone whos inclined to enjoy alcohol would say the same but, a fucking joint man, of the right kind; I don't even believe in such God but I find myself thanking something for it's existence, it's not like it switches my brain off, or on; it's somewhere of a happy inbetween where im relaxed yet I can see reality for what it is and really just enjoy it, like really enjoy it; like we've touched on multiple times; it feels like it's something worth having, like really worth having, no matter what people tell you, no matter how wrong you feel it is because you've said you wouldn't smoke and it's been two months without any, and I've tried anything, apart from human therapy.

I don't see what I could learn from that as the people around me love me a whole lot more than a professional ever could and not to quote my favourite guru but as Ram Dass said, a therapist needs you as much as you need them otherwise their work just doesn't work, friends and love is there for exactly that, love and love, they don't have alternative motive other than to see you "succeed" in what you are going for and not even that, they are there for you whatever you may be, family is one thing though family still just want the best for you, art is not in your best interest, art at the better of times is an experiment or even self harming, it's hard to put in words but some people see you for what you are, no matter what that "are" is, they are there for it and understand what you are doing with "it"

Yeah, I thought we'd get along, more so than being placed next to each other on a camp, R and X aren't even near each other on the alphabet how did they even place us, it's a weird one honestly, I've dreamt of the name Malina for years, I'm not sure why but maybe it's the feeling of the person I've wanted to meet more so than the name, why the name? I don't know, raspberry in Serbian and I like a sweet girl, if a girls not sweet then what's the point, do I want to stay put and write about this girl or do I want to meet her, maybe it's both but perhaps I have to write about the imaginary love before I've even met her…

...and I hate to say it but maybe it's not even you, I used to call my ex-partner Hare and a homage to hare krishna and when I said goodbye that last time it hurt me a whole lot, I knew I couldn't use that nickname again, not that i'd want to, and maybe Malina is an idea more so that the person I am meeting now, which you will not mind me saying, even though I like you, and I have a pack of thin feel condoms in my bag which I am not afraid to use, and I know you know that, I know that you are game though I know that will not suffice, even then, do you want to go to bed and listen to the breaking bad soundtrack? I am so romantic I know, I don't even have candles nor a flower to give you, but I have my eternal heart in this moment which is all or we need and I giggle after an orgasm like a little child, what say you to that?

"Wow, you really are a weirdo, fuck it, literally, let's go to bed River, have your next...with me even though you are a romantic, forget the bed, forget the pillows and duvet, lets get naked and take a swim with a joint, let's see how far we can go out before something happens, we're in south carolina...uhh I mean California afterall have your way with me, you won't forget it you're not on xanax, i'm already naked can't you see"

"Oh I can, let's go take a swim, have you got a speaker so we can play this tune nice and loud, which playlist or album shall it be while we take a plunge, I wouldn't just sleep with anyone but you're one of a kind, you're kind of special let's take a good one of a spin, have you heard this one?"

"Molinaaaa where you going to…. Molina"

"Of course I have, lets take a fucking swim boy"

The sun has just set, the sky is pink, so is her underwear, not underwear, so is her hair, where do we go from here and does it even matter, we're together experiencing a moment of pure bliss, pure source, pure god, if you will.

Malina and River leave the lake, as the sky turns to black, they dry off to 'A horse with no name' playing. "Oh I love this song"

"Man, you'd be lying if you said you didn't love this song, it has such a feeling you can't turn it off, who knows what it means and who cares honestly, what's next? Oh well, I don't mind, I'm glad I get to "work" with you, I was beginning to doubt this whole thing.

"Yeah I mean it shouldn't even feel like working, lets see what tomorrow brings, i'm sure it won't even feel like work after what we've done tonight, and will likely continue every night, or day perhaps, who doesn't like midday sex"

"Well, my Ex, I hate calling her that, she deserves more respect, would say "who even likes having sex at this time, all sweaty and weird, at least have a shower first" no no, the sweatier the better, the last time we fucked was on new years and it was the best sex i've ever had, MF DOOM's death was just announced and I was sad smoking a joint, knowing our relationship was also about to end and it was just the ONE you know, THE ONE"

Morning breaks, 7:30, a weird kind of haze, a little bit cold but in a nice way, suiting as it's gonna get HOT later, she's already rolling a joint but I'm sure she's saving it for later who smokes at 7:30. "Hey, let's get to camp, I didn't even smoke last night, I was too distracted hah. Yeah let's go, I think we can get away with painting signs or something today—that'll be fun though I'm no good at fonts, good time to practise, on the job, on work hours, how much are we getting paid for this again? Doesn't really matter—I've nothing to aim for, it's quite interesting just being here for the time being.

Pockets of dough, full of pockets of air, broken shores and deep embedded shame, painful groans as he gasps for air, he wouldn't even care if he was I, and I don't care for him—someone should, shouldn't be me though i've been left on edge with a level of disbelief of what's even in front of me, pockets of hope with blue moon—orange wedge, on north of viaduct or is that a Y? I can't quite see it's so faded, faded huh? Okay maybe we are and being a stoner without the weed takes a type of will, not really a skill, I used to say it happens on its own, but to who? And what for? If we can't take ownership of one direction we can't in the other, it's the source as well as me, hmmm, in a kind of peace but not yet free, ahhh, as long as it wants to be, not needs, but don't keep me i'm not an animal, if i was, i'd still be stuck back 6 months ago, more like drilled and closed on both ends, throwing up stone sober and walking away straight, though I am in brighton with pink bricks and I don't mean the ones in buildings, still a lack of judgement though, from their perspective, that one's on my plate, though it's more observation placed in thought, I can think—why not think if i can, while I can, child addicts gambling for fake LV key chain bags with 2 pence coins on the pusher thing, "hey how much is this game", no no hold on little kid, im winning, in first place in my teal japanese whip i picked on auto select as the timer was running out.

“Yeah, I like that one, what do you think you’re judging about people? Even if you kinda don’t, but do at the same time.” Malina inquires.

I think it's a kind of trying to understand, the person in question, the universe at large, or God…And I think people know the difference between judgement and that feeling i just explained, being interested is a kind of look but also look away, mouth open but don’t let him see me seeing, judgement is more, i’m looking and i’m interested yet I don’t have the same views on life (I presume, from the shirt he's wearing) so I want him to see me looking, so he/she knows that he/she is in the wrong, does that make sense?

Yeah, I get it, it’s why I always compliment strangers in public, who are just doing their own thing because they understand that it is them and no one else, it keeps them going, they put that outfit on for themselves, and the music they’re playing out loud because they forgot to charge their phone but they wanted the vibe but when someone else recognises the motion, the feeling, the love that they hold for themselves, in deepens that bond, with themself and also the universe, and I don’t think you really need affirmations or self affirmations but it does help, I let others do mine for me as I’m too busy with other stuff and I don’t like repeating myself unless it’s repetitions in art or strokes while swimming, stirring while cooking, I won’t go on, you get it.

“I might start complimenting strangers even if I DON’T like their style, just if they’re trying, or is that counter productive—I can’t tell really”

“Hey, hey hey he-”

“Hey, hey, what’s up, you okay” River says, in a calming manner, panning from a child, to Malina back to the child, making a kind of “oh god what now” kind of expression, the one when a child is about to ask you a question you know you won’t know the answer to, not just any child, a Christian down syndrome autistic one, at that—probably ADHD too with how much that diagnosis is going around, that’s even a cliche point now, if you need stims you need them, not children though”

“What am I doing here” the child asks, mouth dropped.

Oh Jesus Christ, he really had to, didn't he? I know he means it in a profoundly weird way as well and not the camp, it’s never about the camp, how and why did he pick me out to ask this question, for Go- it had to be me.

“What, you mean here at the camp right? Your parents sent you here, didn't they? To have fun, make new friends, new experiences, etc.”

“No, I know why I am at the camp, but why am I here, I feel like I shouldn’t be, i’m very confused”

“Have you eaten today, maybe you are just hungry, we think weird thoughts when we’re hungry”

“No no, I’ve eaten, more than enough, and look at me, i’m fat”

Wow, where’d they find this one, what an awareness for a child, reminds of a 6 year old saying he’ll never achieve his dreams, while doing a cute fake sulk, Oryn, what a child, I’d change his name for the story but I think it’s the only one i’ll keep the same, magical child, led me on an hour long goose chase for his shoes, couldn’t find them, saw him wearing them not even 20 minutes later, I don't even know man, just no words.

“No, I wouldn’t say that, and I don’t think anyone has the answer to that, as little comfort as that provides but it’s the sincere truth, it’s likely the greatest question a human can ask, so congratulations on that, some people never even think of it and it really is a big one eh? We’re born but we don’t remember it, suddenly we’re at a certain age, and we’re just kind of awake right? Playing with a train or something, or getting hurt and reality just dawns on you, you get chased by a dog and your adrenaline just pumps into action.

But really, no one knows, there's theories for almost every other type of question, or just every question, and some questions actually have answers, some come close, but I think the only real answer I can give you is that life is just for that—To live it, “don’t philosophise life too much, it's already complicated as it is” My dad always said to me growing up, I too wondered that, too much, I still do, at 24 almost 25, it’s what’s led to my journey, i’m not from here, can you not tell from my accent?”

“Hmmm, yeah, I should have known you weren’t from around here, you talk all funny, thank you—I guess, maybe I should have a nap or something, everythings clearer in bed, and more so after the nap, so we’re here for no reason?”

“Essentially yes, just do what you think you should, without hurting others, where possible, I think you’ll be alright”

The kid walks away, turns into a run and he goes straight for the lake, we see him in the distance, laughing and socialising with other kids”

“I guess that’s what happens when you tell the truth” Malina says to River, “If you told him some Christian type thing he wouldn’t have believed you for a second, that’s why we tell the truth, that’s powerful, hopefully he doesn’t keep asking us, I thought I was gonna have to have a turn for a second, good answer though, i’m sure it’s just what you’ve told yourself when you’ve pondered the same thing right?”

“Yeah, something like that, I don't think comfort actually does that much for kids, and at that age you are already so smart and sharp, even with a disability—I guess, although at the same time, what I said does provide comfort, because of the lack of it, kids can tell when older people are lying to them, it’s in the eyes, we almost look up for answers when we’re lying, or its a lost look, a scramble for thought, when you look down and exhale and just talk the straight truth it just is the truth, or at least it is A truth, or rather, it’s not a lie—for lying’s sake

We’re lining up at the food court for lunch and I have arrived late, I can still see that some food is out but it’s disappearing by the minute, I’m not sure where Malina is, she must’ve eaten already and gone for a swim or a nap or something, we’re not working until later so—

I bump into a tall athletic guy, he looks peculiar in a good way, as if he has something to say about something but God knows what, massive rucksack and he's holding it tight, he must be around 2 metres tall if not more; "You know, I really dislike outdoor sports, yet it's what i'm instructing this month, I can't really stand kids either, i'm too awkward and they see right through me, I'd rather be on my computer coding right now but..." Oh, this really isn't the place for you then is it? I say and laugh, how come you've come to the buffet so late as well? I don't think there'll be any food left by the time we get there, and it closes at 1. "Yeah I don't think we're getting lunch today, though if you wait, I know where they store the food and I can get us a few bits, you like ice cream?" "Yeah, love it" I say and smile, "Okay good, they have these massive cornetto's in the freezer, if we don't get any food i'll just get us a couple of those"

"How are you so fit and healthy if you don't like outdoor sports? Or physical activity in general."
"I was very fat at one point and I only focused on my work and making money, at one point you make so much money you don't really want anymore and it makes you realise that you are alive and that you should maybe take care of yourself, weird i know, some people get that from a lack of resources or money, the feeling of being alive, but I've been in offices and in front of screens for so long it's like a second person was born from within me.

It's like I was just an android doing my coding and investing on stocks while my brain was developing a new person at the same time, it's like I forgot that it was me doing the work and I was living a separate life at the same time from within my head"

"Interesting, I'd like more money"

River and the guy he just met, Filipino Phil, get to the front of the buffet line as it closes, no one else is behind them, "yeah, no food for us today, where are the cornettos then?" I'm quite annoyed but it was my own fault, I should have lined up earlier and I haven't even had any good food while i've been here, I stocked up on ramen, fruit and veg for late night treats and smoothies and things like that, the food is free for us but the additional ice creams, smoothies and shakes are all at a premium so i'd rather not spend money on those, I brought my own blender, because why not. I'll take an extra cornetto for Malina, I'm sure she'll dig it.

"Give me a sec, the storage shed is just around back, wait here..."
"Bring me two if you can, one for my friend"

Phil sneaks into the storage shed, which is more a warehouse really, I watched him go in, I wonder what else is in there and why he's just opted for the ice cream, maybe so that they don't notice? I'd like some real food first.

Phil comes out with three large cornettos, I've never seen them this big and it looks like they've defrosted. "There you are" As he hands me two. "They have defrosted though, you'll have to refreeze them in your room, fuck, I can barely wait"
The cornetto's as mentioned are absolutely huge, vanilla ice cream with chocolate corner bits, smarties placed on top, a large flake bursting through the middle, I wonder if the centre has that gooey kind of chocolate bit or if it's plain, I don't mind either way"

"Thanks man, i'll see you around I guess, i'm gonna go find my friend and put these in the freezer"

"No problem, let's get to dinner early so we can actually eat eh?"

"Yeah, for sure"

River walks back from the canteen, which is 2 camps away, a good kilometre, maybe they should have given us bikes or scooters or something, this is gonna get tiring, it's a nice distance to walk before a meal though, just makes you all the more hungry, luckily the staff canteen is a separate one from the one the campers eat at, that would be an absolute mess, sharing space with all those kids and people. On the way back River spots some children riding on 50cc quad bikes, no safety pull rope things, "huh interesting, maybe I could borrow one of those for getting to a from camps..." God i'm so lazy, I usually like walking but when its a functional walk you tend to rush because you know the destination, when you're out in proper nature without a destination it feels like you could just slowly walk for days, observing, thinking—singing and such, i'm really not wearing the right kind of shoes for this, i've only brought my jordans and my birkenstock sandals, nothing in between, a nice running trainer or something would have been nice. The ice cream is gonna defrost even more in this heat, before I get to put it in that tiny freezer, nothing in there so far anyway so it doesn't matter.

"Oh she's putting her clothes out to dry, I should probably wash my clothes, I haven't got many"

“Hey, where’d you disappear to...did you get to eat? I just missed it so I’ve got some ice cream as a consolation.”

“The kids tired me out, I had to run away for a bit, did some washing, cleaned my hut a bit, yeah I had some pizza and salad today, it was okay, you didn’t miss much, though out of a whole buffet I could have had almost anything, they had stew chicken as well as sausage rolls and loads of fruit, you didn’t miss out on much with the pizza honestly, maybe the stew chicken if it's there tomorrow, I wonder what's for dinner, what kind of ice cream did you get, did you get me one? You better have I love ice cream, more than real food.

“Yes of course, a giant cornetto, like a –”

“I know what a cornetto is, why’s it melted”

“Yeaaaah we’re gonna have to refreeze them, some guy I met also missed lunch and he snuck into the food shed and got us a few, I don't know why they’ve defrosted so much but at least we have ice cream, big ones at that.”

What a strange guy too, he's a water sports activity instructor yet he doesn’t like being outside nor water sports, it seems that everyone here wanted some kind of change, or were forced into it: forced themselves into it.

"Does he look quite stern and angry too? Always wear a backpack?"

Yeah, you met him?

"Couldn't miss him, I love that archetypal backpack wearer with square glasses, he wants more but doesn't know what strand of more, he's probably picked somewhat right, though he looks quite…rich, based on his composure, he probably could have just gone travelling on his own"

Yeah but I think there's something about having set days that people like, in a school kind of way, even jobs are starting to feel that way, not that I've stayed in one for more than 6 months, but it's all baby talk, spoon-feeding as some of teachers used to say, I kind of get it too, wake up at X time, X day off, X holiday, something nice about it if you are that way inclined.

Speaking of which, what are we doing tomorrow for the day off?

"Huh? Are we not just smoking and fucking?"

Malina looks at River, with a ridiculous side eye, sipping tea

Yeah I mean that's for sure a part of it, boat trip?

“Then we smoke and fuck on an island, how romantic, I like how you think”

Yeah man that’s the one, what Island should we go to, there's probably a few, wake up early, take the one with the least people in line? Maybe, or just rent a rowboat and see where we end up though just the sound of that is tiring me.

“Yeah no, i’m not rowing, we’re gonna have to go into a town as well to buy more weed at some point, shouuuldn’t be a problem though really, we are in America, California afterall, how can they even say Cannabis is banned at this camp…I mean, I wonder if we smell…”

“Nah the showers and pine resin has our backs I think, that shit is smelly…you ever make a coffee at 2am because you can't sleep?”

“Huh, yeah I guess, sometimes, when that I know I won’t be able to sleep annoyance and irritability kicks in and you just give in because the coffee will settle your nerves in a reverse kinda way and at least you can think a little clearer”

Yeah, that one.

“No weed and I'm pretty sure I don’t want any fallacy?”

Yep, i'm just thinking about it now because we do have weed so i'm trying to be grateful in the moment but also in reverse, thinking back, that makes no sense but, smoking a joint while thinking about not being able to sleep for months, mmmm, hits different, I almost have to convince myself that I won't smoke it anymore...then I always refind it, and I thank...something for it's existence, everything's the same either way, it just gives me the ability to slow down for a while, gather my...lost self, recalibrate, i've always loved that it's not a depressant or a stimulant, there isn't anything quite like it in nature, I think most will disagree but it's just not for them, evidently, I hate the stigma and the projections mostly, it's what always makes me stop rather than my own inclination too, you get bored of things naturally, nature finds a way, you know

"It always does, the nature or natural argument is a weird one though, and I know that's not what you're saying but it just came to mind, "It's not natural"---Drugs, etc, it's here, nature brought it about in someway or another, I do prefer the MORE natural things however, oxymoronic but, pills just taste bad, that's a sign if nothing else, MDMA and LSD are odd, you feel at one yet LSD is semi-synthetic and MDMA is purely synthetic, mmmm even ketamine feels somewhat, uhhh, good?

Beneficial? It's a medicine for sure but cannabis feels like coffee at certain doses, or even better with coffee, at certain doses, certain strains. "Cherry picking strains is going out of your way for an addiction" I once heard, hmmm, would you not drive or walk, bike further for your favourite brand of coffee beans, or wait in line for the food you actually want? I mean we're alive after all and I'd rather take it positively rather than seeing it as an addiction, it's freeing, enabling, not in a projecting way like a shitty friend, telling you what you want to hear, no? Maybe you should just do you, I haven't seen you on pills or anything else but when I smoke with you—I can tell that it's you, I've not known you for long but, I sense it's you, from your highest source, you almost can't drop your shoulders back and stop your racing mind, we're not the same, no one is, but we're very similar and I enjoy observing you, you look like a building with the wrong set of tools when you're not high, I mean you're still there but, you're almost apathetic, how would you have responded to the fat kid (bless him) if you weren't at least a little high? You wouldn't have told him to get lost but perhaps you would have lied out of laziness, and you're not lazy when you're high, you don't get high to get high, like you said in your outer monologue, like me, you do it to get by and it's not a drug fuelled frenzy nor some kind of craze.

it's not a heroin addict on a mattress in a corner of an empty decaying room, searching for escape, you're not escaping, you're entering, and you obviously don't mind leaving either, maybe you don't feel love without it, maybe you love yourself more when you have it, there's a love to finding your favourite strain, setting out a

dedicated rolling tray, taking your time, while the tunes play, open up a nug with your fingers and bring it up to smell it even though it's your favourite and you've smelled it over a thousand times before, how long have you drank coffee and you probably only ever do that once in a while? It's love, of the highest order, you even smell it again after grinding don't you? Make sure to roll it in a perfect cone then smooth it over with your fingers, look at it a while, I saw the way you were twirling it a while before lighting it, getting down to the last second, there is no rush when you're in love, you even missed the point in the song where you'd normally light it, naturally misaligned in a perfect way—because it doesn't and it didn't matter, you probably should have lit it even earlier so you'd be high for that point in the song but that's likely how you used to do it and you've forgotten it, trusting the next song will provide or even the silence, we didn't even listen to any music last night, did you notice? You're not scrambling, you're searching for resolution, you want to go forward."
"Wow, yeah, I should just do what I want, as if I haven't always done that, why would I change that now, to mould into an image, I feel like a diluted stew that's begging for more vegetables and spices, as well as a longer simmer"

"Shit metaphor"

Yeah, I'll keep it in though.

"Keep it in what?"

Nevermind.

“Hmmm, fair enough”

What would you say your favourite album is?

“I'm not sure, you know that’s a hard one, you are only asking because you want to talk about your favourite or favourites, no?

Yeah, ill go first I guess, though I do want to know what yours are too, would be interesting to compare, not compare but, you know, share notes, as it were, favourite album takes some real consideration, childhood favourites, timeless ones, not timeless classics...

...I don’t care for someone else's ranking of what they think the BEST albums are, i’m merely talking about my FAVOURITES, strictly, an album has to be like a soundtrack for a film otherwise it’s not an album in my eyes, a random collection of songs just isn’t it.

There are a few, in close running, I think only time will tell which is my favourite or i’ll never be able to tell but: Animals, by Pink Floyd, If only I could remember my name by David Crosby, and probably workingman’s dead by Grateful Dead, a better way to reframe the question is, if I had to pick only 3 albums to listen to from now until death, it would most likely be those 3, let me think for a second, maybe create a top 5 I cannot live without, there are songs I'd love to hear of course but, so many live performances, outtakes, etc, luckily I don't have to choose but it's a good experiment, I've always loved InnerSpeaker by Tame Impala, weird choice, almost cliche but think about that album and how it shaped the psychedelic sound of the 21st century, what kind of music taste must you have to create something like that, what kind of soul, In Rainbows is up for immediate consideration too, immediate, that album is some of the highest art I've ever heard, top 5 songs however, would be completely different, which is weird. You'd think each top 5 song would fit into a top 5 album but it's really not, like your favourite scene from a movie may not be from your favourite movie, nor top 5 perhaps, but the album or film speaks volumes, as a 50+ minute standalone piece of art, It's fascinating the sort of influence the beatles have had on me yet I don't think they'd fit into either list, some of the greatest front to back albums yet, they just live with me, they are almost inseparable, you know, I don't listen to Hey Jude a whole lot but man that song, again, I almost don't even need to listen to it, I just know it, like a rolling stone by Bob Dylan however, on the other hand, would probably need to be in that list, man 5 is too few for songs, 5 albums I could probably do but songs? I've listened to probably 50,000 in my lifetime so far, if not more, random playlists, and by accident, radio etc. I'd have to pick a top 5 live performances as well, now that would make for a great playlist, or footnote for a book. Mirage by Camel might have to go on the album list as well, making it 4, so far, there isn't another album like it, nor

band, quite unpopular compared to other Prog Rock bands, however everyone into the genre holds it up there, it's impossible, Yes songs are almost just showing off for showing off sale, Camel, is full of soul, meaning and feeling, like an even more out there Floyd, perfectly so, a bit eastern—
But not too much, it almost becomes a gimmick when a western band has too many eastern sounds, yeah we get it, you like India, so do we, do something original, kind of thing. Kikagaku Moyo are a serious consideration as well for their creativity and original sound, the band i've seen the most times, and probably for a reason, I'd see them every week, but they've split up, bogus Japanese noises instead of lyrics, what's not to love, they understand that language was a farce yet here I am, writing, in language, maybe through it, hopefully just using the words to navigate a brain rather than...

Maybe I just haven't lived enough to create a top 5 albums, the first 2 are for sure on there, i'm not sure about Working Man's dead, and I couldn't pick just one Dylan album, Coyote by Joni Mitchell may well be a top 5 song, China Cat is 100% on that list, I'm not sure how it even exists it's the purest touch of magic through sound i've ever heard, Cowboy Song from Remember my name is for sure on there...anyway, impossible task I won't bother actually—I tried.

Did you feel like you were kind of above average intelligence but in a stupid way also? A kind of, "this is stupid", "why are people stupid", yet a lack of comprehending what they were teaching you in school...

because..it was stupid. What is that feeling and is it just this huge fucking ego of mine that I know isn't so huge at this point, as i'm broke and in debt, half a bottle of wine in and 7 - 8mg codeine pills 1 tab of 130ug LSD and one pill of mdma in, interesting it is though, starting another shitty job at noon I kind of enjoy but dont know why, maybe because of the necessity at this point? It really has got to the level of washing other people's plates in order to make money hasn't it? I guess it'd feel worse if I was paying rent as well, with other people dirty plates, but i'm not so it goes under that sub-conscious brain tab of "temporary situation" which makes me feel better about it though it's only just begun and I don't know how long it will go on for, hopefully not forever but I doubt a in-house design agency will take me in soon and my band hasn't even recorded it's first album, though I know i'll make it in music even if they don't, I hope and "pray" they do but I know I will, otherwise i'll die in a couple years and this book won't get published, or I'm dead already and i'm not so it's safe to say i've "made it" in music.

"You think work comes first? Pfft it depends what the work is..."

If it's bullshit like this it just takes the back burner man, unless you're excited to get up for your "work" everyday your life is on a back burner, man…

…I know that because when I enjoyed my life it didn't feel that way, I'd get up with a certain kind of non-ego specific reason, spirituality aside even though i just used the term ego, which is kind of psychological as well anyway but, I know I have to do X and Y due to how the world works, but I don't think about it because there's no point in thinking about it, people only talking about their work when its shit work is like people who only talk about news or politics, wow you really are the least interesting person in the room, I almost misjudged you for a minute when you spoke of your love for nothing then won't onto even less, perfect.

If you enjoy your menial job and you have other things than that's probably the best you can possibly hope in this reality, and I mean it, unless you have the heart-mind connection to go out living in a tent, which almost nobody does, turning up from place to place, having faith that you will be provided for in some sense but not knowing how, thats so fucking insane but i dig so much, I only wish I could do that, I almost did, but something always pulls me home, "I'm gonna be hungry" and "what if I don't have anywhere to sleep" Hmmm, they're good questions but.

I'll carry on drinking my wine but i'll swallow these codeine pills with water, because I am healthy after-all, I was sober for a whole 5 days recently and I was sober yesterday so I might as well be healthy, I eat okay and I exercise and I use my mind and I have a social life so beyond the irony I am probably okay, I'm not drinking out of PURE sadness or anxiety, its a side mounted thing like a gun or something, I don't know, though I wish it were cannabis and it shortly will be.

"huh? We're smoking right now"

Oh nah I was just... shall we go to a graveyard? I love graveyards, do you?

"I wouldn't say love but I do enjoy reading the names and seeing how long the people lived for it. I like to make a competition to find the person that lived the longest, we should buy flowers and put them on the winners grave."

How have I never thought of that? Yeah let's do it, gonna be weird asking someone where the nearest graveyard is but it might be funny, it's okay if it's funny right? Say we're taking pictures or... PrProbably weirder actually.

"hey whos that, he's coming towards us"

I don't know..

"hey, either of you got a lighter... "

Yeah man, here, wait what the fuck are you British too? Smoking a joint as well yeah?

“Yeah man, where are you from?”

Bedford

Nah man I'm from Luton, what the fuck.

Rivers head drops in, that way it does when he's in comedic disbelief

I used to live in Luton, shit hole but I love it man, you wanna come to a graveyard with us?

“Don't tell me you used to go to the graveyard at the start of Crawley green to smoke up? “

Fuck off, yeah I did, favorite spot man

“Where's this graveyard? You two a thing then? “

“Hah yeah I guess so” Malina says first.

“Cute, let's go”

River and Malina start walking in a random direction with their newly made friend

What's your name by the way?

“Samuel”

Sam for short or? *Malina asks innocently*

Nah, what the fuck is a Sam, salmon?

Uhh yeah I guess, what if there's a salmon out there called Sam? Sam the salmon?

“what are your names” *Samuel asks back*

I'm River and this is Malina.

“River? You don't look Korean, nickname? What's your actual name”

I'll tell you later *River says, laughing*

They make their way out of the forest, a very long walk but it's lightly sunny and everyone is in a conversational

mood, they stumble upon what looks like an abandoned barn, the terrain has changed from forest to desert, rather quickly.
Shall we climb it? Malina, you good to climb?
What because I'm a girl?... Hah no I'm not like that I'm just joking, yeah fuck yourself I can climb it.
Wait, how are you gonna climb in your birks?
Watch me.
Can I go last then?
You absolute perv, of course.
Yeah don't worry, I'll help you up if you need, River winks and bursts out laughing as does Samuel…I guess I'll go first then, says Malina.

They climb to the highest point of the barn, there's a gap every few planks which they use to their advantage. It's a good 3 metres tall.

Wow, what a lousy view, I don't know what I was expecting, we can see for miles from here, absolutely no graveyard but, weren't we supposed to go on that boat trip as well? To an island. Malina says, thinking aloud.
Oh yeah, oh well another time maybe we'll have to go into town, what even is the nearest town I don't remember.

They climb down from the barn and carry on walking further and further from the camp. We should probably head back soon as it's gonna get dark, River said, and they all agreed but carried on walking for some reason.

St Ynez 17 miles

“Heya there, stationary travellers, whatcha lookin at”

“Huh, just that sign…we have no idea where we are”

“Well, 17 miles from St Ynez” *holds onto buckle and releases a hearty laugh
“What are you folks looking for?”

I mean we were looking for a graveyard but…

“Isn't a graveyard around here boy, I can tell from looking at you, you like those instant noodles, you know they aint too good for ya, I don't need to tell ya that”

“Huh what, me?”

“Yes you, purple hair, you a faggot?”

River laughs “no, this is my girlfriend, isn’t she pretty?”

“She is, I'd keep her for myself…”

“Easy…” River says, laughing, but with a slightly overly protective deep in his brain, he didn’t realise he loved her this much, well, I.

“None of you are American, what's going on here?”

“We’re on a camp America program, we’re at Cachuma lake”

River is cut off by the cowboy man looking fellow

“Ahhh, you’ve walked a way, you’d better head back before the dark gets ya, it will but head back now and it won’t be too bad, everything is closed in St Ynez anyway, you are better off going on a day trip to santa barbara tomorrow, you young folks will enjoy that, I know I did in 67, topless girls, skateboards, marijuana, yes yes and more yes, go to santa barbara, you won’t find anything ‘round here…hope y'all have a good day, I need to get back to my wife
with this” *the man points at a plastic bag, evidently filled with shopping of sorts*

As the Palestine conflict disrupts the social vision of all-rightly so, I carry on writing in this book without an end in sight, I refuse to be swayed either way and I just nod as people tell the details they think they heard, saw or read without reading up on the history of the place, I do care but what could I do other than just carry on writing, in deathly silence or accompanied by my loud laptop fan, that first warehouse paycheck will do just fine, though I do want a good-elegant piece of machinery to lash out on, I've dropped this thing, lost the screws-trying to remove the faulty hard drive, I've sat on the screen bending it almost the whole way back, luckily it hasn't broken thus far—-given the treatment, and well it's a good thing for now as i'd only have my phone to write on, i've given up on paper, I can't write fast enough and my hands hurt quicker than typing, and not to mention I lose paper but this is saved on the cloud, there it is again *saving* with a little spinning recycle sign, please don't recycle it google, this is my life line, I have been playing the drums more though it's hard to improve at drums, given the nature of the instrument, writing however is mainly from experience and experience doesn't dry out until it finally does, I come to a dead end frequently but something always brings it out—experience, doing stuff, hearing a story and adapting it to be my own, it should feel wrong but we all embellish—

—it makes for an interesting story, I'd like to think, I went to my first funeral recently at the ripe age of 25, you would have thought someone would have died prior to a quarter of a century passing but it had no bearing on my life, neither did this one, nor the guy from friends dying today, I didn't watch friends and I don't trust anyone who does or did, okay, I'll let you off if you were a kid, younger than 12, at 13 the sarcasm kicks in and that show is far from comedy, it's a painful drain on a person who really wants to laugh, though everything is overly scripted you can still find gut wrenching laughs if you really look and it's usually by accident, the slightly racist friend who knows the edge really well, the guy who joints random words together yet it fits together like a dyslexic puzzle.

"You're on a roll with your career!" the email says, yes im scanning items in a warehouse, im sure ill be rolling them too, what else could I do with my degree in illustration, anything but draw or paint, I'd rather just be out in the sun with my mouth open like a lizard, licking up the rays and thinking about the next meal, not the next line, any kind, or the next stroke, paintings fun but it's also quite boring when you have a racing brain, I should read more but it influences me to much, 19:11, I feel like its 00:11, i'm pretty much ready for bed but i'm always ready for bed, unless there's a party to go to or i'm in a position of getting high, which might be soon.

This warehouse drug tests but I don't think it picks up ketamine, I know it doesn't pickup psilocybin or LSD but you cant really abuse those for an illusion of benefit as I'm used to doing, 3 day binges to sit and read and walk through trees with slight paranoia but it is what it is, I can't snort anymore however as it's too much a nuisance, no matter how much you crush that fucker down it bites like a cunt with gonerea, or vaginal crabs, or just a cave like hole with those crystalised points coming down from every angle, my Ex's felt like that once and i'm not sure why but it wasn't nice, it wasn't nice anyway but that time it was particularly not nice, I didn't tell her and I just went to smoke a joint instead like I always did, the start of a failing relationship, that's why I tell my dad i'm not quite ready to be a father, and i'm not sure I ever will but mothers usually carry (literally) the first part, and the 2nd, with the dad a kind of manly straight foward prop, am i beyond repair, im not really sure, i dont want to give a final kind of evaluation at this age, and I don't even really think too much it just kinda comes out and I observe and place it, wherever it wants to go really, it comes from feeling really rather than thinking, stems from a place in time, as it always does.

The three of them are almost back at camp and it's passed the curfew by half an hour, luckily you don't have to scan in or anything, it's not a job, it is but not so much so that you have to scan in before going to bed, I really should try the prison food tomorrow, it doesn't even look that bad and it even comes with the mid 2000s food splat mp3, mid2000sfoodsplat.mp3 or something, I wonder what number it goes to. How do people smile so much while working, I wish I could smile while working—working, meaning the absolute fiercest projection of that word, not like—writing this book, working, working-working, I thought drugs were dissociating, I have to let my eyes recalibrate when I leave this place, It's interesting working and knowing the job i am doing is actively being replaced by AI/robots, grab item, scan, put in bag, repeat, repeat, I am home now, this is good, I am too tired to do anything but "*home*" nonetheless, trying to stay present yet looking at a yellow wall with cravings for substances I've not yet tried.

Another quit job, another bout of disappointment I can do nothing about and it's not worth worrying about—7 hours of anxiety for absolutely nothing other than perhaps the anxiety itself, I've been noticing my anxiety more and more recently, i'm not sure whether it is higher or whether i am just noticing it more, coincidentally, or rather, in a well timed fashion.

I tried DMT yesterday for the very first time, a highly powerful psychedelic, one of the 3 main forms, NN-Dimethyltryptamine and it was the single most anxious i've ever felt in my life, and it's the least i've ever wanted to move in my life, coming from someone who is quite hyperactive.

Feelings of the past come to instil, more confusion and distrust in the most trusting time, I cannot wrap my head around the way you stop mine, I'm speechless for a speechful man.

I got myself into a fight with a demon last night, the more i retaliated the more that it won, i got it into a headache lock and it grabbed my chest that's when i said fuck that i know that im done, kicked it in the head and i got out of bed and i lit one up, hey hey man dont you run, im only at your chest back lay back down, let me reach that balding crown and drag you underground, you aint real i said let me fuck you in the ass then we'll see whos boss, stop grabbing at my legs i don't wanna get pegged, settle down you bloody rowdy clown.

2:24 nightmare so real i had to write it down and so i'm writing it down, this vape isn't working let me get a straight, nah let me lay back down and get it figured out, don't grab at my legs hex Dextromethorphan im so vexed i let it pass, this rhymes not worth it i ain't got any style, too many looks now what could you want man, look away and settle down, come any closer and ill suck your dick mate don't make me turn that smile into a frown, your face is reserved its as if your upside inside out like a schizophrenic cloud on a sunny day where'd you see that one it's just your imagination as your a looney tune.
so many girls wearing too much perfume, smelly british carpets covered in items, man there isn't much room, let me call a federale to sort it out, no wait he'll arrest me and i'll never get out, and i don't wanna get jacked so i better keep sleeping to gain some heavenly clout, the shit i spout no wonder you don't want me around, it's for certain i'll get out of this boredom and really align, why can't i sleep i really don't want any loud and i hate it

when the young ones call it that as they don't call it cannabis, i'd live in that plant but it'll send me to my doom but like a naughty kid, locked up in his little room.

i'm so infected i've got ants and spiders but it reminds us that i'm truly alive and i don't want slide on a 90s jungle floom, i've got better things to do im not at a rave, kids in new york snapbacks taking selfies as if its 2008 and who bought you that vape? Your parents must not love you otherwise they'da smacked you straight away, you better throw it in a lake, no wait that's what bins are for though people don't use em, i pick up after you to watch your face so you make a better judgement next time and don't kill our oceans in vain, people don't even swim it's just an act, can you get a better picture next time mum i nearly got my J's wet for that and i can't even put that on the gram, what? Is that a samsung, upgrade to an iPhone so they can control your brain, facetious lines that catch you out and make you wanna stray
and ill leave it that way so you think for yourself rather than listening to what this brain dead half spiritual serbian clown has to say. but i'm not going away i'm friends with my hate and my shadow, i try turn away and that demons back in bed.

Nah sunny jim it's not gonna be that way, doritos and a dip for £7.50 have you actually lost your head i'll walk a mile so i never have to enter that establishment, one of my favourite words and they all laugh at my level of nourishment but i just can't eat no more and i don't want it, the size a some of these humans its purely embarrassing, coming from the national drug ambassador of 4 different classes, my parents lived on rations and i wanna know how it felt, door to door trades, coffee for beans, lentils for cream, have you read they're coming soon and we may be dead? Let's flee and join the harassment, better than a war torn lack of grocery-nothing-to-do no development local enforcing of human sense, that doesn't want us anyway, they killed their own people just to prove they were right, a fascist state worst than 30s Germany and that's today and not back in the past, i better not show my face or my stars otherwise i wont know whats coming when i cross the danube, beautiful river surrounded in trees, politicians convincing seas and masses that people can vote when they're dead.

And what's this new obsession with bridges wheres there to even go in a place with no choice, my triple great grandad built the first radio tower even then i can't do basic maths and i can't even be bothered to take my morning bath so i'll take my coffee to go and carry on with my flow, I don't wanna give them satisfaction of feeding their economy when they couldn't even provide the basics for ground soldiers that made them and here i'm living in pure unsustainable wealth, writing shitty tunes at 3am reminiscing of a time i could get to bed and stay that way, time to eat so i can flee those demos, I want them to come back and tug on my legs so I can carry on writing tunes with hummus to my name, and I want to die in Spain, my soul lives there and it's never left, low in crime, not much theft, problems of its own but at least it's a hot one.

I could go for some wings with sean evans and the dead queen, im sure she still owns a limousine which doesn't get used, the doors burst with children trying to get away from the nonces, they've got machine guns but we've got love, Jesus will come back with an army of turtle doves, and when he's here you'll have some explaining to do, no more kings and queens humble yourselves you're under God's rule, that's not something you learn in school they want to keep you cruel, following rules, it's why i dont smoke weed anymore it's all government crop, if we grow our own we'll face the iron room just for living like humans, off the grid?
Nah they'll whip you back in you need to pay your taxes you can't just live they'll find a law under section C, what does that mean its from a silly book that you read with a white wig on your head, I wanna create a real lawsuit and not through the system, i stand up for what's right, that's what we've been tasked with, we all have to play a part otherwise we'll keep the cycle of birth and death going like that cancer that is eastenders, and it's all a drama, i want no harm just peace for the awake and the sleep, the dead and even the creeps, the ones who have real needs let's help them get better rather than shouting helter skelter, my fingers hurt let me see a doctor, there's no room stay at home and do what you need to do, gather some resources and carry on through, there shouldn't be any gloom, we're so advanced, past civilisations? I don't give that a pass and it's a waste of time. Why look behind when we can be so present there is no ahead. I better go clean my room and get back to bed, it's 03:49 and it's getting late.

I've got work to do, so I better not pretend that I'm perfect, this world we're in is divine however we are living on the surface, lets go deeper and create real love, I can already feel it, it's bursting, don't just nod your head as if your listening, your attention span is proper lazy and i thought mine was a travesty"
Riccardo finds me sleeping in the sun, peaced out like a proper hippy or a homeless bum, yeah I waited 20 minutes for you to come back around, you were out cold.

Was it a peaceful daydream? Yeah I was so depressed I thought I'd just lay, 2 guys awoke me speaking too loud, I look to my left and there's an angel with long hair, face of a soft cloud, awaiting with a smile,
Wow it really was a while this field was empty and there weren't any sounds, it's good to have you around, it's a surprise people like me, there so great, i'm empty and hostile like cheap barbeque dressing, I won't say no it's been a pleasure and a blessing, whatever I ask for I get 10 times over.

I can't watch TV and I hate A3 movie posters, that's what I mean, why am i so preposterous, I think on my feet and say what I mean, i don't shave clean and why should i, stray hairs and young fertility, your objection is killing me, and let the lord be the witness, i don't live in pure strictness and it's filling me with hope yet anxiety as we're all dying slowly and walking to our graves,

Sorta thing where you're dehydrated but you dont even move because the moments that good, you know when someone just captures your full attention and you just couldn't be anywhere else...

sorta person you'd share a disposable vape with like 2 junkies with a single needle, yeah that's an eleven, because 10s don't exist only 9s with hell of a charm.

Spellbound like harry doing alchemical pottery, was wearing me thin, i can easily drink but lemonade or a look of your face will do more than just fine, contrast is the aim but not too much of it, magenta green and pink, there's a whole lot of it and so i'll skip and find a new combination as those colours make me ill unless its specific hues, i hated that jumper on me but it really suits you, a twisted dark purple.
Wishy washy flip flops hot drops with small dogs, they all flog hogs down shop floors vibrantly dressed whores fork out for beef hot tongs lifting scorched scones scarred and marked, it's not a farce, leave your mark-in the dark night park in Abbey church hill, sausage roll too cool for bluffin, I'll just take the lemon honey muffin, no man no huffin in this huggin culture, they're all vultures, they don't want ya, they don't even want Jah, man scratch my back with some wise wine dense verse like ginsberg doomed Kerouac short brimmed hat, arch top Tlaloc staircase fades in like his post-modern suburban lofi trim, resting on church spires, hands of a 'dwardian butcher lost among anti queer peers in an ancient quire, provided adequate roman aqueducts,crack, erupt, spill over, my veins filled with cinnamon swirls fat girls with Yttrium hued pearls living in my head.

let's a take a whirl into the depths of the surface wave rather than play dead, pretend we're ahead yet sleepwalking with a side of no cocaine, just breath and talking, the lethal spirit burns, fuck that and no more toking, weed smoking? You must be fucking joking, grew up too fast yet still left behind, theres no more time to be messing around lets build a musical mosque and burn it to the ground like 9/11, outspoken like kanye with the flow of a heathen, no time for political correctness, theres no hate just appreciative awareness for the ones that create no fairness.
And so I do stay inside my little yellow shelter box, bladder expanding, why should I feel like this, why should anybody? Head, stiff, jerked back and to the left like a junkie or JFK as he got shot, back and to the left and back and to the left, motor parades showing off the new top of the class, it is of course, the biggest farce, mr president, not mine, not yours, then whos?. A motor parade, are you showing your face or losing it? Why would you walk out to see the president? The King, The Queen...They're all crazy locked up jesters, im sure they wish they could be free, Downing street or Vatican city on a pedestal in front of a people bowing on one knee, laced snake embroidery on Gucci's outside an illuminated under-chassis LED Audi,

while people are lost and don’t have enough to eat, and this is all part and parcel of living in a big city, and we have to vote just for the sake of it, even if i don't believe it, even if i don't feel it, the people are fucking screaming, can’t you hear it.

Meanwhile we camp in the rain ,waiting for a family of nonces to be ordained. put a silly hat on his head and leave the taxes, he's above that, he doesn’t need them. How dare you say that there our monarchs, they've done more for us than you ever could and hey you're not even british with your turkish face and your slavic trim

,sucking the governments half-brain-dead policies and laws, the worlds free, whys it enforced,, there is no true civil liberty in this town, city or nation, we are gonna have to be the ones to make them before they break us and turn us into mush, swiping left to right, yes no, yes no, im 5ft16 but really i look 6ft1 believe me, and i love hairy smelly dogs and buying hippy garms on etsy. Have you seen the new IOS features? They’ve really done it this time, wow. This Xbox controller even has buttons on the back.

And I mean this in love and not hate, i just can't tolerate seeing people controlled in the masses. I’m not a christian or a saint, a Buddhist and I’m an Illustrator who can’t even paint,, I’m Ilija for man's sake.

I'm also wrong, never been a fan of big things or girls wearing thongs, i like a little mystery don't tell me all the facts, even if you knew them, it doesn't seem that way, perceived over intelligence is here to stay that's why i prefer being stupid, open ai has a thing to learn, the algorithm is off, its created a living travesty, no one around has much transparency, we're not in a prison yard we're already at the golden gates, been there before it's a little boring, nothing to learn, nothing rewarding, a golden god who gives kids cancer, they must've deserved it maybe they were stalin or hitler, don't take me so seriously i'm only writing a non-prophetic poem unlike Alan, i know its no clair de lune nor symphony number 5,1811 with the cannons and i why would i want it to be, that shits contrived like jackson pollock's liquid pours, oh but they took hours, oh yeah? so does a pointless walk from luton to bedford with feet wet and deers dead, truck drivers honking while i stop to change my shirt and rise the grateful dead, all the kids on fields asking for balloons or now they call them smart whips, what's intelligent about killing brain cells for a few seconds of airtime, to return to earth and you're sitting with a bunch of roadmen in Bedford park.

I open my window to smoke a reluctant but devilish cigarette, Jimi, Squeals with a power riff, I nod so hard I might as well be rolling off a cliff, I close my eyes as 2 gunshots ring off, I knew it was close, too close in fact. As I leaned out the window there's a loud bang, a car had exploded and the smoke was already coming through the window before I had time to close it. God, what a moment, the best part was that I didn't need to go into uni, I don't think i was going to go in anyway but this made me feel great about it, I had to sign in and out everyday; “Where you going” Ahhh just for a walk man, i said “What? At 20 to 12?” Yeah man i cant sleep so i'm just gonna for a lap, maybe brantwood park. Christ what a shithole, I wasn’t even lying, well, I was buying that nasty lemon haze that was always my last resort, I’ve always enjoyed walking behind the airport as there is never anyone there, other than a farmer or two, mighty confused to see a stylish young dissociated hippy dancing with a cold brew and a-toking on a big ol zoot, shotgun shells, pheasant fare the well, you stood no chance, you are now the name of a renovated new-old pub on the edge of caddington green, I rarely revisit that session Jimi had with Stephen Stills in his basement, but when I do…it really does.

Drug addled joy named an illusion, I'm just doubling down on the existing one, I'm sure it'll add up to 21 or at least 20 with a dealer bust, I'll name my son blackjack yet he'll be called by the name brown Jim because he's desaturated about 70% on the slider, drops by 10 every few years, on his 50s they called him milky steam so that really describes his tone, as his skin tone gets more desaturated, the alcohol percentage becomes more, he's not had water for 20 years and he's got no sinks either, or a shower. He used to be a soldier but he realised quickly that killing was wrong, then why do so many people kill and get killed? Declining health, no monetary wealth but he says he's happy and I believe him. You could double the amount he says he gambles then add a couple more. He keeps a bottle of ether he made himself on stand by just in case, no he doesn't wanna kill himself he just never wants to be chained, he's a free man, truly. Women come and go but he only has love for one, how and why does life do that to a man? Life's not teaching you lessons you just pick up on them as you go, if the prior were true we'd never get to live, prepare to prepare to prepare, learn to learn to learn to never use the learned.

He doesn't place much value in knowledge anyway though he is a smart man. Does the mosquito not see that the human is a dangerous force to it? Survival instinct I guess and we're the same even if the surviving gets you closer to death, for some it's all they know. People say it's sad but... Yet.. It's their gold, they don't want yours, they don't know of it even and wouldn't steal if it they could, they have their own and they love it, it's god given to them like a gift of talent to a child prodigy, this is their fame as they don't need fame, in their eyes the lord has blessed them with a personal elixir.

Leisure shower hearts on fire let's walk home so I can devour you, what's that right there, behind your, twisted pinky finger, brown reception in the sky, you've been dreaming so long you forgot you woke up, how was the sleep on the brass frame bed? Did you wake up feeling that you were better off dead? Can you look me in the eye, can you take me out and make me fly, can you make me see the I in I, I'm just merely me, forest swamps set me free.

I always feel like I'm on a train, walking, thinking and turning, stops in 2 steps, but it's a footlocker then a dessert an a kind of coffee-waffle place, should of got a shot of him eating, what a character sadly disabled, that particular burger King is in a class of its own, insects are the main customer, 2 staff and are always hiring, one on grill, one on the till Is probably enough, couple years of living, working, exploring, I moved away but I always come back, I've never tried that burger and I think that I won't, the mall is a circular train with no one getting anything done, same faces relifted same shop stations, that kids eyeball is on the floor, he left it for later, he's kicking his laces until they land in a loop, like a happy child, around and around, just to be around, to see a colour, won't it flood you big river, no I think I can handle it. I once saw a guy smoking a joint in weatherspoons there, only in Luton. There's a real beauty to a place like that, I like being as high as I can when I stroll around to really take it in, a large iced coffee with a joint followed by a beer and a line of ketamine.

Cascading parade, leave them with no shame, how much do footballers get paid? I'm already plain, wrap the cloth and keep warm to prevent cold vein pain, he's still talking, where's the button for his brain, or should I tug on his ears until I get 401 error, pierce a hole through his cheek until he can't talk no further, ending with a smile, he feels really high and proud, thought he'd make the crowd shake, he feels you vibrate and now it's too late, going to bed sober yet feeling eternally baked, where's a line when you need one, I live in a dissociative space free from hate, when you're leaving don't forget to shut the gate, pretending to not project, pretending to be, perfect. And I thought you were— leaving so quickly where you headin for? It's not over there I already checked, the speckled paint on the ceiling doesn't suit the floor, or the decor, bargain bin from the bargain home store or did you pay a whole lot more to be whiter than Taylor Swift singing out of a fake barn door, glued to your wall with a mounted steering wheel filled with old CDs of bands you used to hate, fender should make aeroplanes and French presses, and serve the coffee in 4th class, but first let the pilot take a sip, he's flying this whole shipment of excavated ruins, he's going all the way to the grounds of the Boston Bruins, no stopping along the way, it's alright, there's WiFi, so you can plug n play or drink 7 pink gins but make sure you hydrate, packs of zyns closing in on stimulated zen.

Erected sisyphus I am trailing, arranged pictures of us, unveiled but prevailing, it's a master of tone and cracked syllables soft spoken to the mind of a pagan, even the sunbrella falls to the thoughts of a far out alien, trench coat of a tistic kid in the wind it's flailing, he thinks of himself as a sculptor but really he's crazy, throat gurgles from a distance daily, sunflowers and grapes from his head, he waits with his ticket he's patient, I know that I'm her favourite, I should seek rather than be sought, I just don't like chasing.

Cigarette burns, there's a glow in the window I don't want to stop it grateful animosity tiled soul with a tilted frame, that's when the good comes in, stark realisation, this boy hasn't got any patience, 60 seconds to feel renewed no ill take the hatred, glued to the neck I don't wanna move your warmth is a sensation, 3D characters living in ice-cream I don't wanna wake them, I'm just a lick of old taste in a world burning with false novelty on a axis of rotation, I don't compensate for actions I put across, I don't change my speech or writing I'm not a politician making a statement, carpet coat it's not a radical trend neither is my nasal affliction.

Accept people for what they are
It's the only key to social liberation
Cutting down to a rare slice of humanity
But open to all possibilities.
Ah no I'm not smoking at the moment,
Here take some of mine, you did give me £2, said a homeless man with less than nothing, it's the principle not the weed, thank you so much though, you're strong, keep going man, hes routing for me out of pure love and I don't even know him, I'll go back and give him 5 so he can feed his dog next time. I had a feeling of attachment today, don't let yourself crash, not only will I let myself crash but I'll also ignite and burn, the so called journalists reporting fake news, a social algorithm that serves no purpose, we're one in our division it's only natural difference in experience, don't let it hold you, pretty face like a sunflower unfolding.

I love love, I love giving love even if I don't receive love back, love is life's backing click track, love is the birds that love to sing, love is my brothers having my back through perceived serious pain, loving is the genre in which i play, this love won't go away, when I eat a pizza i love the belly ache, I love my drugged out brain the way I love my sober state, I love laughing at dark things and I love smiling in true cheese, 9/11, oh please. I love being cold so I can feel more awake, I love being warm during a storm, I love a close game of any racket sport as it's better than a stomp, I love hearing altering views so that I can learn, I love watching hot air balloons take off in the air.

Eternal train journey to get a little fix
The conducted said what is that in your hand,
The people all looked n stared
There must be something wrong in his mind to play with the law this way
The conductor stopped the train, said boy if you want that kinda freedom, you better just walk away, okay that's fine, it's the way I want it to be
The day I met Rose, she said give your love to me, I tried it once, I tried it twice and the third just went away.
So I climbed the bus, deal in hand, I'm going for the 2nd round, do it now, let the sunflower grow right into your brain, If he sees you now just deny, I'm following the lord today, if he says it's okay, I'll just pray n pray, the driver can't stop me, he can only make a face. I got off in style, said thank you for taking me home, I thought the man on the 2nd deck was gonna punch me straight in the throat, but when i looked real hard, he had a deal of his own,it's a loving you can keep, it's a loving you can keep, you can keep as long as you want, you don't have to join my fleet, it's just a song about trains, it's just a song about planes, leaving expectation at the boarding gate, at the boarding gate, at the boarding gate, I'll wait my turn when I learn I don't have to hate this world, oh when I learn, I can love myself someway

Fallacies erratically expressed from misplaced intent, your the one who asked me a question, I can't leave now the worlds not stopped, I don't want wine from the basement, clinically diagnosed, that bitch must've gone rogue, the sliding door doesn't fully close bounces from side to side like a Hollywood nonce on a low vibration, amphetamine laced burnt toast gross slow roast pig brain upheld by the clock like face of a man that knows no pain raining biscuit crumbs, he beat up a nun for the way she treated his sister, glasses off to cry as if it's hard to talk, the 21st century mr Jones asking stupid questions, dead corrupt cops, he'd have rot either way, pushing for war neither can afford, why can't it go away? World wide forces aren't here to save us, world wide forces want to blame us, the temperature is getting high and we've been here before, put em in a square suit and send them to work until the government bills are paid up, control is an illusion do what you want don't take others projections, if you stand your ground lousy flip flop opinions change as if your the one with a big brain not the educated scholar, how do certain folks get their kicks being so deathly boring, are you gonna start living your life in your forties? I live in hazardous chaos from day to day, I don't need to grow. It happens on its own, it's a measurable science easy to deny if you don't look in the right places…

...stunted expansion is sad to see, lack of sociality in your younger years, old opinions stuck in your head why not speak bravely, my boss is this, my manager is that, but how do you feel inside? No feeling from the eyes, straight to bed after a functional head and a dull filled stomach with no hopes of change, it might already be too late, too emotionally spent living to work on bullshit that barely pays rent, how can I not resent it? I don't feel human how I get talked to, I don't stare to get stared... No it's no use and it doesn't matter, I carry my heart highly but I see others dragging, smile to a frown, am I some kind of clown or jester, how are there still racists when there are no races only flavours, can't imagine a world with no ramen or Italian coffee, Belgian beer and Chinese robes or japanese folks dressed in nice clothes flowing down passed the knees, incredible conversations with a man in a park from a place you never knew existed it's blissful, it's the foundation, people still shipped and locked in basements, it's painful, that's an understatement, wrapped in barbed wire and thrown in the river, or trapped between boats without choice yet we risk our lives to climb rocks for a million views or a sponsorship for new socks so we can sell our souls to Satan, 32" in front of your face so you don't have to feel, distract ourselves until we pass or you realise your lives been wasted on stats and figures that get wiped with a click, I guess it's the same as beating a drum with a stick but who talks to god through a monitor or a TV?

Everyone's an artist or a creative, everyone has suggestions, some let it go wild, some let it get shut down, insecurity or traditional parental greed, man I wish we wouldn't concede.

I am not one for prophecy, I am not one for a cold window sill of addictive spontanaity, the moth seeks liberation, we are already liberated, presidential candidacy is only for true menaces, a plaster won't solve your problem, your 50/50 glass won't attribute to much, we're all in a rush, even if we walk slowly, somethings need pace, this is obvious, the world will end when the leaders have had enough of false leading, the social scientists are paid off, the gap in our hearts may never be filled for we always desire, killing desire is desire against ourselves, ice tea is a necessary berevage all year round not just summer, too much coffee hardens the mind, although lucid, we are all still blind, but you can buy new ones if you have the money, people who drive cars with a serious face make me laugh, like smoking cannabis without laughing, though everything is funny if you look, the world is on fire but so am I, I won't be put out by a pail of water, you'll have to drown me, I swat flies then feel bad for causing death, petting cats is therapy, smoking is an unhealthy luxury yet I feel no remorse nor should I, ginsberg said poets shouldn't get involved with politics otherwise they turn monstrous, luckily, I am not a poet.

The greatest love story ever told, on a kind of pre-earth plane, away from 21st century fast food and garish buildings, what was it you were looking for? You've already got it, deep in your heart mind, it's all, I in I, no climbing nor a steady chase, I personally don't think it's a race, we're all heading in the same direction, I forget that sometimes and... Lose myself, I know that we're all good, though we need villains sometimes, I see you for what you are and that is I, and when you see it from another's eyes, it's quite astonishing, it's naturally, stoning. Floating in a transparent sea there's no transaction, love is free. The wit of fruitful trees the divine carries and settles, I used to think cows looked bored, now I can see them in me, everything gets eaten in a way or a few, oh that look from you, the way I stare around you to not get drawn in, she's a muse, she's a rebel, she's an outcast, it never... I think it's in the details, I'm always in the deep end, I don't walk through shallow water, I always get stuck in, as if I'm eating an orange, but without teeth, what does that mean? I see a rowing boat lost in a muddy river, drifting far from the bank, grounded and centred by a stone, never seen by men, it's more a myth at this point but we know it's there, I think we all try to find it at some point but I'll keep looking, I think I almost had it but it's just too dark to see, I'll bring a water flashlight with me when everyone goes to bed, not to hide it but it's when I find my zen, if it is I won't sell it, or fetishise it, I'll hang it on a chain, keep it in front of my bed.

Yelling yellow yawn yearning yet yodelling yugoslavian young yach yin yang your you yesterday yeah yacht twinkling twice then thrice, thinking that they then thought, taught tough things thoroughly, tongue twistingly torqued thermal tights, thanks to originally orange oracles orchestrating oligarchs of Oregan, officially out oiled ocean obviously oatmeal okay, and a anarchist anticipates Algerian apples allegedly above all atoms, atmospheric alarms additionally afoot attributing alimony around Aberdeen, attentive appalachians approve apparently, evidently evolutionary excavations eradicate elevated ears especially embossed evening Europeans embarrassingly excluded ecstasy extract embargoed Ethiopian emeralds emergency excavation epistemological error encapsulates entrapment, pretty personal paradise pretended pleasing personality pure pear pairing pen pulled pork primary purpose pentagram pending payment pendulum pleasured pine pain painting pressing pencil porcupine perverted professor pink praying praying picking pumpkin pie pieces picturesque plug pushing purple haze having hated Harry's hard hell hailed hollywood horchata harassed hood hip hop hippie halal hoppy harness hanging haribos Harlington hippodrome heat holders hopefully harmless humming home...

…Long length lessons lessen leases like love livens lifes loud lobotomy lake leeches looped lucky lunch later lingering London laboured laboratory labelled lended lava lamp linking Larry's licenced location last, bring brown bread baked butter beans beautiful base bad basement beneath bars both busy bat's barely bothered by brunette brine brilliant beet beers battered beef buns but bigger bitter bulb burns blood booked brooding bars because binging babes barf.

Running from boredom through aggressive noise, silence points and ponders on refined themes, imagine listening to music through a dream, or answering a text killing the steam of the story, my legs only hurt when I rest, I've recently caught smells and tastes through my lucid ability, the silence deepens things you thought you knew and throws it for a loop, negative thoughts arise and you can correct them, hills and graveyards do it for me, graveyards on hills really, especially far out flowers begin to sprout, songs find meaning with the lack of bombardment, well, my brain begins to sing on its own, it does feel like it's about the journey even if it's a wasted one, that feeling of coming back home and... Expecting something, it was better to just be out wasn't it? What's the nerve that says come home, come home, I want to be alone but... I kind of, need you, even from a far. Let go of your vices for a month and they're sure to come back, they want you too. Leaving without a phone, which way is back home now? What was I even thinking about? Nature's bed, why are they talking so loud there's no need to shout, it's just...
The details always excite me, due to a lack of big picture though I do hold one in mind, I just seem to be soaring even if it's slowly, I sometimes dream of joints and lines, never the other kind, which says a lot, I'm stimulated enough, it's quite easy to spark, battery running low is all in...

Looking through a windowless frame, it's always about writing, the meaning escapes me and that void can be quite frightening, it's exciting too, but it carves out a chunk of my soul anytime I try to strike gold. I sometimes starve myself to see what I type, sometimes overfeed until I feel ill, drop the coffees from 4 to just sip to see if it makes any difference but, it doesn't, my computers always journaling, even when I'm not, sometimes takes a forced shut down to really reset the browser, I'm sick of schemes and marketing, public lack of service announcement pumped out, when nothing seems to change but only does for worse I'm happy there are happy folks despite it, I dig transparency and appreciate those who have it, I talk through illusionary words but the message I think, is pure and I don't get the point of building up a society that lacks human spirit, human rights and free speech while we're at it. All the great things seem to get ignored for replacement facets, what even happened to love? Nothing through nothing, only stories of trauma and big men crying, keeping the conversation going, getting traumatised more, talking of real work being done through the eyes of a lucrative cult how long can this go on with the divided groups filled with secrets, why do you have to be exclusive to be inclusive at a price that's not reasonable, all the facts are on the table, we're not stupid we're abled, no one even helps the poor other than influences for views...

people projecting about healthy food yet staying depressed, stats of exercise are for yourself to see, I really couldn't care less about your brave transformation, if it makes you happy, take it and run, meanwhile I'll just take the sun, meanwhile ill talk to the people that get no conversation, begging for a human touch he yelled and scraped my finger, he didn't even want money or a cigarette the feeling of skin sent him to heaven, he started in a swear and broke into a smile, what kind of feeling it is to be loved. Everything seems to be an illusion, I feel so mentally sick, my mind wants to puke not my stomach, what leads to these extremes of thinking, morning mania, nightly... I'm just empty again, not in a Buddhist way, worsening symptoms, I can't think or feel, keep the suicidal ideation away, it persists, a flu for the brain, I shouldn't think or feel anyway, it's troubled turmoil, when will I go away, when can I stop pretending to be okay, no writing will solve me, I've come to a dead end, living a false dream, please God, save me.
Amen.

I like his style of writing, it's uhhh easy I said, acting slightly... Stupid, if you will. Yeah you could call it that, compressing her lips in a kind of, higher than thou way, letting people ``win" reveals the serpent in people, an intuition to stay away, be cautious. And I don't need to win, that realisation is enough for me, in truth the writing of the man I was speaking of was truly profound and only easy if you don't read between the lines, a man with the best of gurus, a man with experience more than instantly gratifying superhero films. Acting briefly stupid uncovers the greatest of judgments from people with shadows not so integrated, unfamiliar with the law of projection yet it's their karma they're experiencing for we only experience our own and it's against morality to interfere with others. Fascinating. Anyone can be a guru to any single person in any situation, a homeless man was mine as well as my father. Firstly the homeless man, parking up next to me in a wheelchair outside of Hatter's news, "You're just a poser you know" he says with anger. Okay, that's fine I responded. "you know what a PP is, that's what you are " he says. No, what is it? I'd like to know,I said. I was waiting for cannabis so I didn't mind talking to him, "permanent poser, that's what you are"

Oh okay, that's cool.

"You're an MM too, you know what that is?" no I don't what is it?

"your a massive moron, that's what you are"

Okay, that's cool as well, why not.

This continued for some time, my lack of answering back is what broke him down and he started talking of his life struggles, I could feel his pain. With a severe shake he pulled out a box of cigarettes and dropped one on the floor. "oh for fuck sake, uhhh would you mind getting that for me" and I say playfully, why would I pick it up if I'm a massive moron to you, why would I help you? "

" oh if you're gonna be like that" and he leans trying to pick it up. Don't worry I said and I picked it up and handed it to him, while taking it he touched my finger and that feeling of skin sent him straight to heaven. He broke into a hearty smile and laughed, here take a cigarette... I'm sorry about being rude earlier.. I just... No no, don't worry I get it. In that moment he was my guru, and I was his. Who knows what kind of situation a person is in, this is why kindness wins.

Farting the entire flight because fuck everyone around me, and again. The elasticity of time always fucks with me but maybe the leftover drugs in my system on the flight here made it go by like nothing, I feel the minutes go by this time other then about 30 of them. About the 17th fart so far, I've not been counting however, the sort of jackets some people wear just pose one question, where did you even get that from and why is there a rubber band around it,its looks like an advert for sparkling water, walking bubbles they'll call it, because he's a walking billboard. What's even caused this gassiness? My stomach feels like it has an egg boiling in it, I wonder if you could boil an egg in your stomach, no. Imagine boiling an egg inside a kettle, you'd have to run it twice. Egg in a bowl with cling film over, microwave for 2 minutes, or you just boil an egg. The plane is dropping in altitude preparing to land. I am still farting, I better get all of these out before I get into my mum's friend's car, I don't want to startle her. Let's hope my bag doesn't get searched, I don't have any drugs or anything but I have incriminating 9/11 sketches. I saw a weed crumb in my sketchbook too, that's at least 1 minute behind bars.

No more fueling the depleted brain, reheated self raised grain in flowing braised vains, alpha male on a beta release off beat trail, he's sick of frowning when she's no longer around him and still certain downing of half gallon drums, he's found him, at the corner of a farm nursery shop, horses in pens, I pen down lawless embarrasment flossed through gapped reafs, coral shaped teeth, my boy get off the streets, he's not real, tail foot down the estate stair prayers, selling hyms and flared cheese mix to run down highs, the feeling that doesn't go away, the trails of planes exiting through the drunk pale ale foam too sense to weigh on a scale, keep your body sled aled like fabled ether poison, I'm not proposing hell.

Getting knocked out of my self proclaimed place in time by an unexpected interaction, I don't know his order, don't do mine I'm not a drink miner, he'll wake up feeling a pharaohs ring if he takes the prescription, written, ketamines dissociative hit doesn't make writing easier as one would expect, you more see what not to write and it is most of it, no it's not
Something about alcohol creates a few pages everytime though, and masturbation always accompanies it, especially if some kind of pills are on the menu.

Stick my dick less head on a hotel roof and call me saint, stay off the provincial tile rimmed swimming pool horse hoof kicking old southern slave owners, porcupine ribs glazed ape straight remembering back when the times we're fond off, younger than the 60s stones doored on, folding ripped cigarettes back on themselves so they hold up, ripped quick to the light head, bright face heats up a morning glory stem, condemned all rain through the seeds sign. *

Prisonesque canteen, with every flag, halloween decorations and a best costume competition, I wonder who won, it was yesterday, clear the webs and put the tree in, some roads already have the snowflake lights. People should steal them, and resell them when people forget about Christmas, I passed the drug test so that's good, late boss is fine by me, she did look at the test weird, interesting, I think she threw it in the bin, slavic leadership, why are there 3 of the same tea and coffee machines and then another coffee machine with a different decal, at least it's only 30p, probably nasty. Noodles in the fridge, disgusting, what is there to even talk about with the other human scanners, human forklifts, humans on wheels, few other kinds.

I think that humour is the only way, it's the only form that cuts through absolutely everything and really everything. I'd rather be sad than shallow, the shallow masquerades as important, please give me attention, click the box, get it removed. Reacting, selling them, having them stolen, anything but feeling them, anything but living now, rushing through to leave nothing, and it's derelict, it is.
2 rick and morty t-shirts in a row, differing prints, didn't look the type, other did, greasy n all, beauty is the only way, because if you can why wouldn't you?
This guy has been standing up almost the entire flight, looking at the same piece of paper the whole time, must be quite interesting, wish that was me.

When the depression eases,
When my mind stops freezing
When the world makes it easy,
For a bit
Then I have a passivity seizure of speech
And I'm back in it
The skies blue but perceived as grey
It rains from my brain through my veins
Until it goes away again and I pray
That I'm cured
But I'm…

Who's that singing over there, I thought I heard a word or was it a tune? Who's that singing over there and can they turn it up, I can hear her smile, yellow like my favourite knit, orange will come back when I find the right strain. The smile breaks as the tune changes, she's had to come back to earth for the interval but she keeps strumming to keep the tears from falling, 400 denars in case--- she's made enough for lunch, her coat reveals her true identity, it's sunny but she's cold, blows her fingers between songs but then loses flow, shakes her head and flicks through her thick song book, boring, boring, just played it, rips those out, I have to LOVE them she screams while scratching the strings at a 45 degree angle, self taught goddess of the falling snow, she knows no more than the loss of drab the songs bring, the sunken stream of thoughts go down to a pin and leave them there.

Skies are bright with the reflected fear, oh please... Devil in... Reload the magazine, red down to a lesser one, red not I read, Certainly a bitter chance.
Certainly a bitter branch
Certainly a better way to...
It's not certain if I can... Though
I can't walk you out in the morning sun
You left before it began, and that's that.
Child basket of pearl type varieties, flowers bestowed, front row, don't take me back, the cores rotten and it's hollowing out, my fingers have an imaginary bleed through psychotic hallucination, along with falsely turned faces, ghastly expressions, and a faint dribble leaves my last strand of facial hair. People talking... I don't hear a word they're saying... Don't leave me behind, he really did care / mind, I don't mind mine, but yours.

I just wanna look at someone and smile
I just wanna wave the wand over your head, oh flowery, you don't need to shake me off, I can't spell the word your thinking off, don't say you're tired I've seen you run for miles, asteroid rabbit, in the grass, she looks at me and smiles, takes the wand and it vanishes like it came, our loves a long lost game we return to when we remember who we're thinking of, don't spite me, I'm not frightened, I'm already falling and I can't see the light again, try it nicely, try it kindly and you will see... An open door, he opens, and looks for more, the devil in red startles me no more and the games you play don't bother me anymore... She wouldn't dance or wave even if she loved, loves a dying game, we remember why we came for the name, that escapes our lips at night but the feeling remains, the painful present shakes more than flowery, shake it flowery, just don't forget... You knew me.

Inclement weather ahead, delays delays, a hour or a glass or two, it's not much in the schematic feelings of things, how can I drink straight whiskey, that's concerning, tastes quite nice too, sadly for my reflective, future proofing state I tend to stick around in like a broken circuit spin cycle, those university wash-machines, tri blend whiskey like in the dream I had, very self predictive however I've combined two, what the third one was I can't tell but it made it, wasn't cinnamon, or just pure sugar but an added note---so good I spilled the shot. Very concerning but at least I enjoy one drink that actually gets me there, not gets me there like the lysie-ke-nnabis trio, mckenna said the psychedelic experience is as essential as sex, id argue the lysie-ke-nnabis experience is as essential as sex, I wonder if mushrooms would do the same but they are so souped up it might as well be mushroom skunk, i'd love to measure the psilocin content of plastic tub mushrooms compared to natural liberties, those tub apes made me feel like I was on a candyflip but without christ leading the orientation. Is that Bryan Callen over there? Ah no it's just a jew. Same trim n face.

Trains and other modes, I'm in the field of transportation and I mean soul logistics, passing on of divine goods, what was the weather like when the iron was put down and what songs were sung, you'll miss me when I'm gone, all the folks have long been home, fire from a kraken furnace to roast the stewed bones, carve the padel the right way, left from right, take the old folks some getting used to, chequered sky with a 2011 emo balloon, the cuffs scrape the floor, luckily workwear, yeah workwear, hard cotton twill, it'll hole up but it'll hole up nice and I'll look like a...

Catching that last wind, last train don't stop there, the sign says thee, well I'll try again tomorrow, he says as a pigeon breaks the silence around me, yellow pigeon, like a yellow cockatiel but less yellow, a lot of Yelling…it's unsettled.

Rumbling old rock of a man torn shirt brown down tumbling, right foot tight left not so much and where's the break but also what's the point in it... Taste, yeah I guess. What was her name again? I don't think she had one in the first place, Corona? Surely not, Karina. You meet kind people everywhere to never meet them again and I don't know how to feel about that, you know people 20 years and they're not as nice as someone you knew for a week and a half but then people have layers, though in a hellish realm being caring is intensely difficult so props to her, no one asked her to be nice to me. Yahe Yahe Yahe, some words sound better than others don't they?obviously. A man dragging a wheelie bin behind him as a suitcase, storied man of culture of course, luton borough it reads.

The cold lingers, fingers, holding tightly, holding to the container containing intravenous alcohol, not literally intravenous but when you think about it, it may as well be, if said person keeps sipping, as in, it's a complete noun, drinking, he's in a state of drinking, nothing else could cross his mind, as when someone says to you at a bar or pub "you drinking tonight?" To what metric I replied, a double shots like half an espresso in alcohol terms, yes I am drinking but home and not here but there's no point they might as well call it alcohol garnish. Old folks blowing home, give them a reason to find some time, in the fields of no burden, it's just tossed aside, the real turning, for the feeling, it's a revolving petal flower growing and that's stolen or passed on.

I only know how to destroy in my life, when nothing is left til renewed and I couldn't have it any other way, virtuous oh, apart from all the cattles that I have listed,
If it wasn't a quick confession then it was distressed, mid air arrest and I can't feel my toes no more, sold the settling on nothing more than average performance, throwing the joker in when it counts, where's the second one he yu gi yoh'd it too soon, too sharp with no tools shedding jingle jams baked even, skeleton elastane from a tombstone suit wearing, nodding down the vertical line for the pixel paradox fractal theory it's grown too long and has greasy rhined edges, raging, too separately he looks up a god at confesses, it's the last dance on the last train home, willingly content sips brown down to the powder, refill her.

The characters come alive in the evening sun, just before it sets and the airport winds blow cold through the ariel rush hour-no take off after 12---better get it up in the air, flights are a strictly Buddhist activity, as are airports, shopping with your girlfriend and sitting through an incredibly boring conversation on a very specific subject, I'd rather share a wheelie bin as a flat but as I said, it's Buddhist "training"

Primark with your girlfriend is probably the most egregious breach of free will a man can endure, they've done a great job at creating a generation of clothes returners.

Sometimes the thought of an alcoholic drink makes me utterly sick, I guess it was 9am but the way those cans of blonde lager looked at me, I could feel my stomach crying out for water. Have it.

It's all good planning until the day comes, not enough of this, I need the equipment, where's Bill Hicks when you need him? It's getting too serious around here. Why would you collect those---there's a recession or something, prescription, economy, an autonomous state, what day do the pensioners get fed, at this rate I'll be the columnist for the beds on Sunday, a somewhat sad county but maybe country, it was just 30 miles out I caught some peace, shotgun shells and the screeching other side of the barrel, less people, warm trees, a frozen lake and a farmer's dog.

No use in dissociating no more, I can't afford it, I'm not an Alexandra road bum stoned cold more smacked frozen, 7% if not more tin in hand, ready to put up a show but it's no luton, it's no bury park, it's no, behind the police station area, the secondary graveyard, odd sightings as with all of those experiences and one would think it's god spurring those moments if not for the knowledge of that 5ht1A receptor being taken over by force,---it's an acidic stick up, pass the joint, remember cannabis is a precious resource more so than a benevolent narcotic---the peace should be greater and will if there is no near fall, it may be a slow fall or an abrupt lesson to be lost and forgotten by future civilisations

I stop by the city centre, rainy day and I wanted to photograph or video, always is and I'm hungry, hire expired and I want to go home, we don't take cash, that's okay, the free breakfast bap will do. I'll get the coffee where I enjoy it. I'd rather go to Starbucks than most bespoke bricked up neon magenta and green plant wall establishments. Bum activity after bum activity, free refills on coffee on the cheapest first cup you can acquire and 3 in and I feel like ginseng ginsberg, because I had some ginseng before hand also, vibrating on the prime ministers lap or just by it, just by it and I love the heir of importance of the politicians pulling up out or in to a public event what would they do without Me oh glorious and I would love to switch places utterly absent mindedly and do some damage of my own oh oh graciously facetiously I'm not a puppet other than my mothers of course and I still manage to cut those regrowing octopus like sticky strings she throws down---ceiling attached like one of those gay blanket dance shows and it may be fun who knows and I know it to be, I should learn to drive what wanna be edge of life beat can't drive, i'd probably be in a grave in marrakech or Floogerville ATX by now..

...why do gravely ill people go out and spread their misfortune with the masses, a cough that sounds like a noise band warm up and the singers not had his ginger tea nor double knuckle shuffle life stirring explosion, so you must have sympathy for him as he is backed up, no pre gig tequila as he's on a liquid diet and lashes out and the xlr cables on stage, biting through them like a diamond miners dog, why can't I see, he exclaims, I took my seizure medication before the mdma, grrr rraaaahggg, he throws his chocolate milkshake over the guitarists daughter, and the guitarist pulls a machete out of his 6ft trench coat, "what then", lucky lazarus, the first guy in the story, aims the stage fire at guitar Guildford, pulls out a 500ml of lighter fluid and launches it Guildford, "your mum", L Lazarus says he watches the quite frankly shit guitar player go up in flames, Basement Ben's fallen asleep behind the kit due to the laced lean he was sipping literally all day, and smoking very questionable cannabis, "it's just my spliff man" he's got 3 shades of the 3 Rasta colours, spread across his outfit and ends every sentence with "Jah know it man, ahh" the ahh changes depending on context and sometimes he'll throw a wicked on their or a simple sick...

The entire band and fan base has had enough of him because he turns everything into a reggae beat and he won't shave his head which ruins the bands aesthetic, he says it "looks very white nationalist" he wanted to get his unmusical black friend into the band just for the image, he even came up with the name Bassy Bahama Sultan as his stage name as he was from the Bahamas but looked Turkish. He played one gig where he played a bass sample on every one, including gills, so it really sounded grand. The ketted out horsey lasses didn't notice anyway, one girl, in an almost heroin like state said "show me how dem fingers move" Autistic and fragile the fake bassist made mouth noises while plonking his fingers in a bass like position, "oh dear" she shrieks and falls directly backwards like in a cartoon, the next horse offers him a bump and he says "yes I do like horses, so this will be quite interesting"

"are you gay?" she asks him

"No"

"then stop talking like that"

They get to the disabled bathroom on the 7th floor, I have no idea where they are but I think it's that skanky club in Milton Keynes, which doesn't make sense but the band was offered £65 between them and dinner.

The powdered horse liqueur was grey but finer than an Asians pussy so he thought why not try the grey walking coma sauce, it turns out it was Ibizas infamous pink cocaine but it was so old the colour stripped away and stayed on the bag, he asked the lady, Sherbert, her name, "what's in pink cocaine"
"everything but cocaine actually"
"you told me it was ket"
"it is ket, technically"
"am I gonna die?"
"Only if you take more" Says Sherbert, as she sniffs more wet grey crystal, not sure why it was wet but Sherb said she had a horrible incontinence issue, the smell makes sense now.
"how about some action now?" she says sticking her tongue out like a deranged horny tik tok teen, pulling her misguided branded jumper over her seriously massive head, he just wanted the drugs not head. "no no, that fake cocaine has got me good I should get going"

She presses a button which locks the door and pulls a gun out, "this pissy pussy getting nomed one way or another" as she says that her finger presses play on blondie's one way or another, drops the gun and does another line, I ain't no whore now come here bass balls.

Fried chicken morning after no remorse from her side she did him every way she could and he hasn't left his house since, welfare welfare, but hes used to Mayfair and this girl don't even do flowers, far from it, enchanted by trauma he just sits looking through his window, almost looking for her but hoping he doesn't see her, mental torture, luckily she didn't have his number, he was special as he was he didn't need sexual violence. Square frames in a time of round, super dry hoodie and dryer than office humour, he's the chair of the board, for office humour, he excuses himself to his coworkers before going to tell an offensive joke, it wasn't offensive and nobody laughed and quite frankly he should be in prison.

The coffee kinda hurts my inner lining but at this point it is free so I put up with it, it's interesting having so much steam then losing it, constantly regaining and losing it, i feel sorry for my family I don't deserve such love, i'm merely an animal, an innocent, mentally debilitated animal but an animal no less, and not that I feel seen any certain way but that's how I feel people see me, "ahhh, bless him" I personally feel no self pity the pity just arises and there's nothing that I can do.

Softly spoken the elegance caress me
Stated fate with no surrender
If I make it through
God has blessed me
Absconded fate taken by a step
The birds still stand and wait
Nothing is moving
It falls like clockwork yet nothing is moving
Tired and unknowing
He waits for movement
But it's not the first time...

He died without knowing.

If only the cold didn't scare me as much as it did I would have froze a long time ago, he long forgot the dream
He long forgot his aim
Aimless, he has no heart to pray
Long lost feeling... Slipping away
Filthy bourbon smut, legs of a race horse, face that screams yes please, drugs keep me fit because I walk to get them. No I don't spit only, clear my throat, to sing at times, not when I talk - it doesn't matter what I say now.

Windflower grow, I used to study this song, LU1, 2nd floor, sandwich bar - - - which filling is gonna fill me up more? Did the hole in the nose hurt? No and a can of coke, I feel more green in blue than blue in green, I'm the green in the scene, I'm often felt but not scene, like a spirit, I might as well be writing in blood the way I write poetry, writing is a part of my addiction but it also frees the guy from living that way, there's a separation, like between church and state, River flows through me and dives me deeper, I pick him out on a 99 cent grabber machine, leaning into social embarrassment, to avoid surreal truth, I don't believe myself half the time even if it is the tune, to dedicate my life to art is an utterly stupid thing to do but completely necessary, Bhakti Bhakti, come back to me, shakti shakti no, exuberant fields of rising technology, we aren't technology we're divine plants in wooden planters, grounded, should he be a machine or should he paint? Some people just like moving, no matter the direction, as long as it's movement, all wasted on the first few steps, not accounting for the last dozen, dozen not a few, take it, put it there.

Rehashing old media in light of... False novelty, false yet it still pushes the heavenly placebo vine, it is really false if it works? And what do you mean by works? It's as if we all have our own book of ingrained definitions, is there a person that doesn't feel the warmth of the sun?
Objectively hydrated,
Hyper Objectively, spaced out
Subjectively, looking further in...
The hoover rings lines of heightened madness, carpets should be burned and rugs slam-dusted outdoors, every town is Luton in disguise, keeps coming and going as my head comes on and off the pillow,
He still only knows one
He's lying otherwise
Blue in green
Yellow in orange
I could sit and watch you blossom,

I now feel a forgotten strain of surrender
I'm no sunflower…

Sunflower sutra, angel of a human, begonias run through her, the missiles are still falling, I'm overdrawn, the nation is out of draw so it makes no difference, I buy draw in place of sitting still, I am the death that comes out of modern fashion, the moan of isms and professional-ismers, it should be, shoulda been, they, ayahuasca, them, temple laid out chairs, deeper damage in the turning from sun to moon, cardiac arrest at the face of liberation, sharing pain I can lose coin for, it's all abysmally perfect even in this way, I can't go to war I'm not 18, I haven't even worked yet - where is my effeminate husband to bring the turkey home, sciatica nerve, vagus soon, no fear---i'd rather stretch in this light, I won't grow stiff, I'm immune to it, there's nothing to be gained from either side so let's *

A far out letter to Jack Kerouac in the year 1959

Smooth walk home, I can't even remember what I was listening to but one of the songs made me happy happy rather than happy sad, I do love happy sad but happy happy only comes once in a while and it could be anything, the chirpy post lady always makes me smile, whether it's raining or 35 degrees she's out there, radio 2, music, questions, stories, she's laughing, she's joining in "oooooooooh good morning how are you sir, you know you always look so chilled" - With a massive grin on her face and that's how it should be, wherever I see her, smiling, talking, singing - It's why the post is always an hour late but I don't order drugs online anymore so it's not really a problem, she single handedly used to be my drug dealer, without knowing; how very very perfect.

Is this level of obsession good? If you ask any kind of medical "professional" they will of course say "no", it is not healthy to be obsessed over anything, these people, not in a negative sense, look like they need the most drugs of all, not even that, it looks like they are on more drugs than us all, talking about obsession, the psychiatrist who prescribed me an SSRI as well as an SARI (a discontinued drug class) looked as if she was falling asleep at the psychiatric wheel, "okay yes, what's the problem, oh yes i've seen this before"

"Do you find your creativity is an issue when you are depressed?"

"No, it's always there"

"Okay, well I think you should take this very CLEAN medicine, its the CLEANEST medicine with very little side effects even though in 2 weeks you will have absolutely no sperm and you'll feel dizzy in sunlight and you'll actually lack motivation more and what you really need is to GROW the fuck up and get in the sun and eat better"

If only she said that last part, I know that's what helped but...sticky toffee pudding in my shoe, okay.

I JUST WANT THAT TO BE MY LIFE ALEX, DON'T YOU SEE, POETRY, CANNABIS AND ALL THE HOES WILL COME TO ME BECAUSE OF MY SLOUCHED COWBOY HAT AND I'LL BE BALD SOON BUT IT DOESN'T MATTER...CHICKS DIG THE BALD WEIRDO, THE COCKTAILS WILL BE TOO MUCH BUT I NEED A PROP I CAN'T SMOKE INSIDE AND I CANT BE CAUGHT SMOKING OUTSIDE AS I'M NOT A SMOKER.

And...

This life long feeling meltdown will not ease and I cannot do anything about it, once again, I wish I could analyse what causes such a feeling but it just makes me delve deeper into the abyss and it doesn't feel too positive, as when I first started writing; I was just pouring out my deepest sadness and fears, it took a while to get through the thick drama to get to something interesting, interesting to me at least and perhaps others if they relate, it might be why I like adapting my own life into fiction, as I kind of escapism and wishing, dreaming-dreaming in a good way I'd like to say, a kind of what if: what if I could own a jazz bar and be my full "character" I dont want to be a character; River—Ilija, it doesn't matter and neither does the cowboy hat, I don't represent anything really but hopefully my words bringing something to someone, they do and it's always a feeling and a look of interest with no further questioning…I guess I wouldn't question Charlie Parker if I could, I probably wouldn't even talk to him, just a sax player at that time though Jack knew of his imminent Buddhahood, I love that word and it might just be my own, I'll let others have it the way Jack termed Beat/Beatnik, I'd like to start my own scene, I am starting my own scene of a tightly curated set of writers and poets, mental—have it alls, I want '59 again, not again like i'v experienced it before but the feeling and the uncertainty, we're at our most uncertain now yet the art doesn't reflect it—

it might just reject it, pussy pussy puss—okay cliche, what then, is there really such space for a scene, monday-tuesday-suuunday, nights just remember the vaseline the milkshakes stick quite strong and it requires a shave or trim per performance.
"Hey you missed the 45 degree angle"
"Yeah, well i'm not performing tonight, you're seeing things, my 45 degree little wing is there to try something a little new, like wearing all black in a good mood."
Wow, beer really is nasty when you don't want one, why am I even drinking it,

And it's 85 degrees, we might as well be in the...sand sauna.
And it's 105 degrees, are we in the...sand oven.

...135 degrees, are we in the sun...sun

No matter which way they try to go about it, the people observe and they judge in the observation, no matter which way they fence it, the people stop and stare, it's a new type of person or an extended archetype, I've seen it first hand…2 lines, 1 shorter, let's go for the long one, I don't know what to do when I get there so it's better a wait for a while. This nicaraguan isn't a 5—strength, it's all the same, Brazil: Yellow-green-design, the other ones: their own colours, whenever i drink nice coffee and smoke berry cigs in doors i remember my chinese Ex, the dancing police guard and she wore a postboys hat, unsuited…for me anyway, £120…to look bad, whats the time mean to you anyway? Is this normal to you? Woah, locked in me in, tight

How can i vow to vow to vow, in this great time of uncertainty the man on the bridge looked like he didn't even know his own name and I want to write like a Allen or a Jack, its that pressure that turns me off of the arts in the first place so I just do it my own way, i've always loved the accents across massachusetts so maybe that's why this intonation works for me though I don't want to copy but it feels like it's me or at least he's possessed me.

Though a hardened alcoholic the spirit of Kerouac goes easy on me—maybe for that very reason, when I do drink I do but sometimes a beer will just do, I just prefer not—drinking, sorry uncle Jack, or it feels like he guides me not to, I can't explain quite how and its absolute lunacy, why do I talk in his voice in my head—do I find it that comforting? And I think I do, there's a kind of...story telling to just talking, and speaking a certain way, and I write about trains and bums, nearabouts far out characters spreading their glee—or misfortune to passers by and I wish to say get an instrument you'll learn it in a day out here, you could save a lit– no...I have to empathy for the street folks of Bedford...I wonder what i'd name my Jazz joint, it would have to be good and it's staying put so no rebranding.

'The Kerouac'

Enough said, no expanding.

I take my glasses off when I eat my ramen no misty lenses here only sinus cleanses, It's my main meditation don't interrupt the noodle monk while he's praying, rehydration for the starved hung over tongue stung, voice broke, if you can't do anything within limits you shouldn't do it at all, as if that's an option, hoping for all, not trying to fall, sprawl crawl, frolic until im 7ft tall, uh, don't interrupt the egg fried rice guru, naruto of big bowls, 2 inch thick specks with rainbow grains, is a passion like a good sinus cleanse already empty, I couldn't empty further, empty my dissipation of misplaced affection, not love, crushing ice too loud, how do you do it quietly to do it at all, it's all falling over the counter—the owners friends on the front row—shirt n tie—are you getting married or a seafood platter with amateur mixology, it's taking a while, we're untrained it'll take even longer brother and you ordered 3 for 2 and it's buy 1 get 1 free, ah sh– I forgot again, opening on a deal as if you're already going outta business, fake flowers so you don't have to water them, full price bottles of red wine, how are gonna make any then, dragon shaped whiskey or was it gin, £50 prize for selling one of them, he's already sipped it—what a fuck, wasn't gonna sell so he just tucked straight in, who's to blame him—
muslim made Bacon, non-halal, yes i'll take one, better than the rubber soy and maybe it comes from G–, no please, i'm not shaken, insides are sadly stirred, rotated on a rotisserie from Best Kebab, that place looks like a strip club, it's never opened up and the owners just play

pool, smoking their own shisha, no wonder these places fall and burn.
Discolored nicotine, stained—pocket, the must of a man in a terminal blues, terminal insouciance for all, escaping—at terminal speed, which terminal is the plane taking off from, if only I could remember, the nicotine is making me dizzy and 13% sick but i'll carry on using it, what is a writer without his nicotine, I miss my straight cigarettes, I miss my coned joints, I miss people I shouldn't miss, I'd rather not miss my flight with a check-in staff member looking all strange at me as I scream at the ceiling, looking at the a380 through the glass, "You fucker" No visa you can't fly, no visa—on the ground when you land, I didn't know I needed a visa, a quick holiday to Luton airport, far from London, it's not London Luton, but who would fly there if London wasn't there, in the name, I bought a £1 pen for £3.50 in a WHSmith's because there was no smoking area past the security point, pubs and lounges, coffee and restaurants—no place to smoke, that's when you change, when it gets in the way, 2 hours of waiting, then 4 on a plane, if we made it, one of those metaphors life gives you when a relationship is ending, along with the plane crash nighmares, what is it with planes? Trains don't crash in dreams, I'd massage her legs across my jeans on train journeys as she'd get annoyed from waiting, what are you waiting for, we'll get there when we get there, London was your idea, for my birthday, Korean? Sure, can I have some of yours though?

I didn't know what to order and preferred the smell of your stew when it got here. Oh no, that was not for me, oh jeez, yes please, oh dear, I'm full. Ah man, can we go home now? I'm tired, set off late, back on the train before 6: commuter frenzy we could have avoided with some patience, England's big apple after all there is stuff to do, she didn't want to. Sitting—rushing through a beautiful gallery, "I'll just wait here" as tears dribble from my eyes looking at a painting of the entrance to Venice by boat, I took that very same route only 450 years later and a whole lot quicker, Venice stinks, nowhere to sit down—why are people so quick to point out the bad, before the good. The place is a gallery and museum wherever you look—all at one.

I came home earlier from university, a cancelled workshop or something, or I didn't wanna go, either way, I step through my door and up the stairs I go, to make disgusting instant coffee—Nescafe Azera, or did I already have a Costa cold brew, no I think it was the disgusting instant with about 7 spoonfuls, FULLS, not quarters or halves. At this point in my smoking career i'd never chain smoked 2 cigarettes even, never dreamed of it, 1 was always enough, or 4 throughout a day always did me; but on this occasion I had a pack of marlboro golds, for some reason or another; a special kind of, not a treat…

Cigarettes are not a treat but a workingman's chore, or a university student's penner stretcher until 7pm hit as that was my call time for my first joint and first conscious song of the evening. On this occasion I lit one up, sitting on the sil, mentioned before, plenty of headroom, and then some, God—I loved that sil, I sit and cry about it sometimes—one day baby, and a better one. I was waiting for my partner to get back from working at New Look, 10am-6pm or something like that, maybe 8, I think it was about halfway through that gold, I wasn't even looking out the window at the point but straight at the glass, and the curry shop through it "don't park here" good I wont, wasn't intended too, Jesus man. I heard what sounded like a gunshot, oh i've heard those before, must be just be fireworks, another one immediately, bang bang, explosion, where to look, straight out towards the end of the street near the black gate, as I stick my head out—the smoke was already coming in, Jimi squealed a loud riff as if he knew it was happening, he probably did, I rarely listen to Jimi but when I do, someone tends to die—if not my soul weeping and asking how a man could play like that, in this instance a real live human, erupting in flames with the accompaniment of Jimi and Still's trading riffs and licks, the timing was bizarre, it was maybe my 2nd listening of that particular jam and I was planning on saving it for that aforementioned first joint slot of the evening but I was feeling rather free having been let out from Uni so early...

You couldn't write it nor make it up, within minutes police showed up, hours went by with news cameras panning their attention to the crime at hand, a police knock at the door, as if we knew anything, I guess we lived at the start of the street and I was just chain smoking golds enjoying the adrenaline, never felt anything like it, i'd say i hope i do one day again but maybe in a different faith, the man didn't deserve to die and nearly my favourite weed seller, I reluctantly call him a dealer though he self-admittedly said he lived as if he was in GTA "Yeah G that merc was a write off, curbed it, couldn't take it to the shop—too hot" Okay man fair enough, never even knew his name though I think it was Dion, I overheard a guy say it once, spider or whatever his nickname was, creepz no, slimez, no—I'll remember and come back oh it was trickz, great name for someone to have when you're buying drugs from them, it was a shit one, coming from a moving river with wonky feet. But yeah, as I knew who did it, "Hide the weed, Harriet rightly said" good point, I don't want no beef with these guys, though they were nice. 4am, my usual waking hour after an 11pm cookie dog sundae hitta and some kind of squash or something, maybe it was just water, I don't think we even stocked squash, maybe she did but I don't really know, she liked summer fruits, so probably so, you know.

There was a little roof hatch and i'd smoke my massive 0.5, looking at the federales sleep in there cars, 3 parked on the street, every which direction, I found it funny I could see them but they couldn't see me, even if they were awake, which they weren't, they probably ought to have been otherwise what was the point of being there, just a call of order, be at the place of the crime or something, as if the gang would come back, the guy was already dead I mean what more could they have done? How did they know the car was gonna park up there? Did they follow them up Upper Wellington street west? Always found it funny how that street was divided in 3 parts as if we were living in New York or something, nope, just Luton town, one of the worst parts but not Bury Park.

You were a different person last summer
I thought i'd wait for you to come 'round
But every night and every night
I just knew there was something wrong my
Sweetest compassion into a senseless morning
The bench stood waiting, so many cigarettes—the ashtray's broken, the birds
Were crawling down to see; what was happening to me
You can trust 12 or 50 and my heart cant take 51, well
My hearts a cathedral straight from heaven, when we climbed up to
The chamber floor 'n fell n dressed in front of the lord above
He's deep ensconced how could you lay your body down,
no ones impressed by breasts, no even admires your wilderness
You're running from happiness my love
You're running from the God's grace my love

You're sleeping while you're waking, my love
Your spirits sick, comes across as weak, my love

But you're a queen, I know, you got your point across the shallow pond...

I'll leave you in peace but let me be free, i'm a walking sickness
I'm a walking disease, I couldn't be free if I tried
I was born sick, and i'll die this way, no diagnosis will put me at ease
Or rid me from my scarred sacred mind
I don't compress my chest nor puff it out into the clouds
I'm spiritually blind through this loving compassion no one can heal
A wounded man, no lover will suffice, i know that for certain, I can
Feel my burden create resistance, loose tension keeping us together
It's not enough for the little boy inside, I don't talk of heart break it's
More a death of the man I could be, before it's even arrived

You're running from happiness my love
You're running from the God's grace my love

I'm tugged and i'm pulled, but I can see straight through
The muddy black river I was once deep in, it gets lighter at points

But stays rather dark, the bench has cracks and is rotten at the
Core, you can't call yourself a woman, it's not fair on the rest
A person has love for even the broken kind, this yellow bulb light
Illustrates a vision of you, I couldn't see before, nor could I learn
What I didn't know before I guess that's why they call it learning
He knows 7 different types of knots even still he can't tie you down
Nor would he want to, he's enamoured by freedom go fly toward the sun
Don't get wet on your return down to ground for you do have to come
Around, everyone has to come around, cracked aluminium foil storing
No goods, just a temporary cure for a thing that won't go away, Bobby
Couldn't keep away his visions of Johanna, or whatever he meant by that
Pre-divorced a year before it happened, self-fulfilled prophecy or the lord
In action, either way the journey is sweet, man it's so hard to get on

Though one day we'll be free in one way or another, I can't stand tall like
A church spire, I'm not an ordained zen priest I am zen itself, as we all are
Life, not in or about it, the leaf, sheep or the land beneath it, my girl goes
Home today and i'm not off to the navy, I'd quite like to save it but i'm not
In no film, i'm not the director i'm merely looking through a lens, maybe distorted
Maybe kaleidoscopic, twisted in a drug infused frenzy though realer than the realest
Reality anyone could possibly see—it's not a drug, it's a way of being, i can feel it before
It's in my dome which says it all, the mind creates what it wants and that's the way of being
That's what's freeing, i'm not down for no fling, i'm not around to be tied with strings, and i'm not fleeing i'm merely around for the wake of society the spiritual or funeral kind, i don't mind it's all the same my love, it's all the same, a look or a rear view mirror can't reflect the true reality we're in and it never will, i was naturally born a sinner so sinning is what I do best, with the brightest intention that someday it'll turn to miracle, I can't grow gold or sleep with whoever turns up, a vibration is a holy thing and it never goes away, and how much I love you has turned around today, in whichever direction, yet I don't mind, love is as they say, blind.

I'm not the kindest kind and i've been too kind, kind to a point of self-neglect, kind where a person with no regrets creates a reason to have them, kindest kind, or has he lost his mind,it's hard to tell if he's sincere when he's so kind, how could you be so kind, kind. Rhyming worse than a rhinestone cowboy in a mask, and he ain't got none so who does, 13,000 white tee shirt wearing clones, washed clean at least, a revolving door of sweat infused tie dyes, crying eyes, I couldn't be me even if I tried so I'll pretend i'm the cool stoner from across the street even if I haven't got the weed, almost as if I have an image I have to keep yet i don't try, still cry as if im lifes ending, pleading heroin induced suicide as if it's time to go, go home, i'm sick of walking all tired and on my own and I sang the song promising i'd never walk it, sucking up to heroes as if it'll help, i have -4 mental health and even less money if they were skill points, it's a trance it's a loop, it's a trance it's a loop—stooping down for permission from people I don't really know and never will, I'll never sit still, never refrain from popping deadly pills until my liver bursts and i've only got one, at least i've got 2 lungs - so I can breathe fine, drudging up a hill as if its quick sand rather than letting the ground lift me grand, forcing sheltered love and care as it's true, it's a spell not love in the highest source, common ground.

My girl is going home today and i'm stuck in a house, merely bricks and nothing to keep it up, dry walls and a dry throat, can't keep it up for long, so i'll let it come down the way it wants to, though it only wants to go higher and higher grow smaller and smaller like the stupid trends i'll never catch onto, clubbing on a substance is a certain hell, snorting on my own is definately much better right? But in a fiendish way I like the burn or is it the certainty of a dissociative high coming my way allowing me to disconnect my muscle from my bones from my membrane to the whole in my ego i'll always fill with stupid lies I don't believe myself, I don't belong in hell but somewhere slightly above it, somewhere where it's rough and it tugs with two beautiful eyes saying goodnight, I can't lie until i'm alright it's not real, my anxiety is not the way that I feel nor the major depression, putting symptoms in a box to get a doctor to order you drugs or staying in therapy for a doctor making too much yet we don't choose our reality, we pick from a handful of choices left to the last second until an answer comes out and i'm not in a rush but I move fast, slowly on the surface as it gives of intelligence, I wouldn't show the true stuff to those undeserving, like black tar compared to crystal white clean stuff, the junkies want the shit kind, I'm so kind and I shouldn't, being so kind is what tapped me into this grid i've built for myself...

While others are talking about a non existent matrix, just go watch the film if you need fiction don't project a false reality, I envy those with faith or religion, I wish I could switch off but really be turned on, to what is here and now, Ommmmm, ding and a crash cymbal, simple chords and choice of words better than mine, more style, more know how, silence on command or demand whichever word fits better, so whichway do you want to go my dear, stop saying I don't mind, i'm as transparent as a green carlsberg, head thicker than jamaican stew but spiced like kimchi just in case I need to pour out and pickle those who serve me, quite deservingly I haven't got a mind of my own, I let those around me think to save me non-existent time, and i'm probably doing just fine, or at least thats what they say, when their not the ones selling their soul on ebay for basement chemicals that run through their already broken brain, making things worse knowingly for no reason, applying for jobs just to say hi and bye, sorry maybe next time—I'll be a chef, who can't cook, following slides on a presentation or read instructions from a book, hey are you okay you look tired, yes i'm fine I just have insomnia, maybe the routine will get you into some nice sleep, no i've never tried that before but thanks for the solid recommendation, like people who post books on their story as if someone's gonna read em, taste of a rusty caravan - not that i've tried one, which cuisine is that?

Give me one of those instead I'll post it on etsy as a bespoke piece of vintage art that'll look nice in the garden just behind the garden tongs, barbeque prongs, 7 pair of thongs all drying, highly acquired, I don't want big things just a life where I feel like i'm living, if you haven't got wheels you might as well be a bum yet i'm thankful for my feet and walking so slowly I could topple to the side of the A6, any minute, he's not too quick yet what am I rushing to it's all the same destination.

The new warehouse worker looks odd, I mean— You could say that about anyone, especially new starters in this specific role, instant interview, pass the shitty little test and you start pretty much the next day, so you can imagine some of these people—of which I am one, you could write up a character synopsis quite easily and probably be quite right, that guy looks like underneath a mushroom, like that weird texture—that's what he looks like, you could push your hand straight through him and he wouldn't mind, I bet he's call Martin or keith, I've always wanted to know that one guy who's name I could never remember so he just accepts what I call him, even just a few years ago I could never imagine forgetting someone's name but as time has gone on and i've met more and more people I think i'm genuinely starting to get to the limit of the name hard drive, faces I still remember most of if not all of, names just go in and out now, unless I need to remember them, even my new manager—Karoline? Kamatta? Something like that.

This new starter has a beanie on underneath the bump cap - like a hard hat but a bit lighter, or a baseball cap but heavier, that won't last long, the cap causes a central migraine anyway, I couldn't imagine adding another layer, you'd think he'd have safety shoes on his first day but no, most people don't, I see "Bring safety footwear" and I assume I must do so.

A full 50% of his face is terrain in acne, almost painted on, it's quite remarkable how 50/50 his face is, line of blemishes—evidence of picking is apparent, straight down the middle of his forehead and subsequently nose, it even breaks up his moustache and beard, I wonder if it's a medical condition or if he is just unfortunate.

"What's that you're having for lunch", I asked, I really couldn't care less and I can see his tupperware but maybe it's even shitter than what I'm eating, "hardened pumpkin soup with garlic and char grilled scampi, missus made me a salad but I said fuck off I'm not a turtle am I? I am bold though" *absolutely abhorrent laugh plagued with pieces of acrylic like pumpkin falling out and somehow upwards*
"How do you harden a pumpkin soup", I asked, squeezing my face so as to not spit my own food out. "You just leave it mate", the way he said mate you know he supports a football team that's not in the top 10, ever, not his local team either he's from Cirencester outside of Cheltenham and he's a derby fan, tattoo of the old mascot, faded underneath his ear with the year and a pint of beer.

“Alright then”, I said. Go to bite my pork sausage I brought back from Croatia.
“What would you say your favourite pint is if you had to pick one?” he says very very loudly, startlingly. “uhhh, just a cold ipa man I don't know really punk ipa or one of those other bullshit gay can ones with skulls and hairy legs”
“hairy legs on a can, what”
“yeah I don't know man I don't really care I prefer weed, I could tell you my 10 favourite strains easier than beers” I say, slightly not annoyed but maybe bothered.
“nah shouldn't smoke that stuff, bad for you”
Shakes his head and digs in to his skeletal pumpkin soup with a fork, garlic sprinkled on top with his grey metal operator hands, the scampi goes in once he starts chewing, or should I say shattering, the soup is now in tiles and looks like mosaiced mosque ceiling but only gross, gravy jesus I'm gonna call this guy, how are his hands so dark on his first day?

I didn't even get to share any poetry with her, I guess because she wasn’t real. I probably wouldn’t have even liked her if she was real, I mean, what a freak, god I need some water why do we do this to ourselves and I mean we, prolonged suicide by dehydration, helplessly gasping for mild sparkling coma, the powder sparkles, at certain angles.

The young hippies manifesto from an imagined taxi.

22nd century blues, you were never normal so I won't be too
If the box lost flow and the head dropped low
You'd be begging for a joint outside my door
If I couldn't have coffee anymore, it'd be delivered on angel wings to my floor
Don't you say that
Don't you feel it
We could have, even received it
But you wanted more

I could see the man in the morning
Come down for corn flakes
A fine tooth Cameron
Pale cream today
It's Corduroy for dinner.
And a pint to listen to old freaks.
Is he really…listening?
I don't mind but what's the point
Leave me alone if you can't traverse the internal bridge, when it's so easy, i've lost sympa—i've lost count at how I feel and that's a good thing, i'm 25 but i don't focus on my feelings, Raseta feeling is a different man, beard rather than tache, ew, and those clean shaven gay ass lookin arab and maybe jews, no swagger on the UAE front, Orthodox jews looking…

And when i'm driving my eyes are closing
Please please open
I can't see
The windscreens broken
Oh my me why can't I
Oh you me why can't you
And when im sleeping your eyes are open
I want them to be
Your my guardian
I want you to see
The words im writing
There all for thee
And when he's driving
I'm just listening
He talks the truth
I exhale and listen
Round and around
I don't mind
And he slows the hasten
I count the clouds
He talks to horses
What's his name
Some kind of taxi
Why was it a tune
It wasn't
Appearing people,
All disappear the same.

The young hippies manifesto from an imagined taxi.

‘A Christmas in Ikea’

The poet starts the beat, the people don't know where to eat…

He ash’d the cleaned-steamed-pocket held cigar, external strap embroidered fix up, pattern…off teal, browns the winning horse kind, the dark have always been quicker, rolling jones, third finger…can't bend,it’s the table for the roll, hairy fingers…obstructed the last sausage and close, it doesn’t hurt but he can taste his own sick from the burning unwashed finger hair, shaded, turq-waved, 20 mph lamp emitted hue, self furnishings are tacky unless you’ve paid in excess, IKEA should be a military fighting centre for battling customers as they get ripped off, meatballs fly, miss, because i'm a turk descendant jedi; I could have been a logger or a miner, my shoulders hurt anyway,if you prayed to…be disabled, would you be.

The rolling shutter closes, post-main-door corrugation.
My girl went home along time ago and my house still stands,
I miss her very much
I talk to myself in place of her…reflected…
Napoleans, only stronger
It’s no holiday living this way
But it makes me feel a certain extended play.

It's been improv so long-the scripts have forgotten the print, intentions only go a certain way if you set them up right, intentions are only okay if they're the right ones.

A pail from the rain collector
Stooping an inch lower
Feathered cherokee sun gaze
Backing hollywood scene
By windy grey by bed town blues
Becoming what you're not
Better put a bearing on it if you can't afford a jewel
Still then,

I wasn't pretending to be a forbidden fruit.

No sympathy, straight to the next provider, it wasn't for him it was the ketamine-bless him his family and the heart---do you know anybody else he was my friend sorry ill get along
I meant no harm only high
I'm merely trying to get by
Aspiration is so high
Drive is a neural pathway asleep
Until a sudden peak
Pop
I'm, the man who woke up
In good time
It's time to sleep

Sleep for real in the conscious retreat not the nightly curse. I pick my disease each week it's not my own we share it...
I was looking for the man who found it
No man will help the pathway deficient
Self chosen...
I don't.
Reconfigured, my computer knows me better than I do, I don't really know anybody, I probably ought to, I know everybody, it feels that way, the people that I know know me…

I'm like a tree, though no wisdom from my mouthy leaves, I could drink more but what would it bring, I can't even get high anymore and the peace I dolphin in spring medit- I'm a monk with lizard skin-don't pet me ill be your pet... I'd take you to be my lawfully.... Pet. I have no use in walking, I just hurt, I have no use in laying, it just hurts when I move, I keep writing, nothing to pay the bills, the words of my past keep me crying and I'm moving on, I can never be the one who learned in the important times others lost in, it's not important, I've lost dolphins, I can't see the oceans... Feel your hearts breath, save from my death.

That was dramatic but…

Spiders and friends, newspaper on the advert page, loud extrusion from internal tones, my stomach disagrees with the days plan, but it makes no change, window no longer opens for his manned hands-beads fall as he enters, shrouded in alpaca like an eastern dame, it shoots me back, i'd rather write an essay on ox than eat your...illegal priests driving stolen fred durst esc hursts, I spend most of my time at work praying to jesus, unseen, i'll hold my tongue, the broken dream of the drunken wharf nodded with a mood of cherry, his calmed mind says no to the low commission on soul. Jesus nods back, "this is the cost" I know, I pay it myself, and it's not forgotten, aa.

Marooned, discontent
I don't want to call you anything until it counts
Or i can bare my own rent
Syllables line up, behind the yellow line, safety is…Unnecessary, green
Military, waled up, woken up, flashbacks
Can't come down
Sharp green fields, in areas
Brown-dried, carrying
Vlatko.
The moment you catch your grandma
Pissing outside, between the wall and van
I only saw her because I too was gonna gonna go
"What are you doing out here"
"Oh my friend is coming" i scrambled
Right, wrap up…it's cold.
All of those friends I talk about but never see.
What friends?
I wasn't born sick
I was manipulated into it
Among my favourite activities;
Scratching my ass and eating cheese pancakes
Not at the same interval
Diaze-dizziness, rocking shoulder and
Buttoned pocket, after market
3 numbers off on the hex grid
Pantone…I don't know.

Valentines through a creeping rose vine
It is mine
I thought it wasn't but nobody else climbs
I didn't mean for this to happen
I'll take the fire exit
I have no game
Just the feeling of the world at once
It's not echoing now
It's not even silenced
I wonder who i'll be thinking of when the pain resumes
I don't think the light was a light
A deluded orangutan'd frame with no substance
Yet im loaded
I'm not asking for more
I did receive it
Email checklist like office suite-
In a closeted round about misfortune
I was curious
Sometimes rewarded
Left with warnings

I can feel my liver through the lens as I watch it back. Did I drink that much? Calamari mistaken vocal liver i'll take the whole platter and 2 kinds of fries i got my mind set straight in an unchristian liking I don't mind i come alive in truth i provide
Others hide
That's fine
There can only be so many sources of light
I am not one
I have no prophecy
Be kind
And I'll provide for thee
Don't pretend you don't see the writing
You only make its sight once
It's turned off, timer was on 39 not 43, my vinyls still spinning, ready ready, she's not ready for me, i wish was i was ready for…skating in the city park, vans, dickies—coat draws him apart why can't I float through oh opio-haze I want my clarity but draw me great desire who trying to find married and get wife would write that? Mmmm.

Flowed trough of the evian grand
Handed to hand
This time yesterday it was 2pm
And it's 4pm tomorrow
Where does the time go?
Perhaps
She don't know
Slavlje ala rio grande
Hola, di si kad te sunce…
Finds you…Dolina
Ko to tamo peva?
Jel je Malina?
Lindo girassol
Del
Thalaj abid

Wasn’t it just the same
I couldn’t change it
The swept left all the game
I couldn’t play it
The rules constantly changed
No rulebook
The man without a name
People’s hero
Awarded a title
Discarded
This isn’t enough

I need a triple glazed sandwich
To wrestle with in the air force
The sins grace
I never felt it so strong
Latin dancer like a fan in my eye balls
Skip tre for the right feel
Crowds skaal
All the lost foam
Paying banana dividends
Am I being misled?

It’s the new beat generation
Free jazz like free verse poetry
A lucid manifesto
We’re all conducting
We must all say grace
The parking brakes don’t work
I talk to hoodless silhouette
He doesn't know

To be beat
Is to find care

To be beat is to find a lavish curry on the side of the english a6, tire shop, window apostle apologists, apocalyptic in their glare, Jehovah—you, I've found me, I don't need Aaaa.

Find the sausage if the curry isn't lavish
Which road was I on when I found God?
Will he still be there as my shuttle gets in?
Does god wait for technicians mending wires?
Or the cable car of the wide atlantic?
Swinging to windowed screams
Graze
Halt
22.50
Somebody's gettin' off

I barely saw the trees, I was looking out for bears and bigfoot, don't tease me. I want it to be seen, can I ride it the other way, maybe I'll see it then, oh...
I could wait forever, as if I haven't already been doing so
It feels like forever when you go this slow
What is forever and who's his foreseeable father?
Am I taking the tram or did the tramadol split
When I don't write I breathe
I can't look for words
They find me.

I'll never stop
Anointed jazz joint
I don't write with a ball point
Not the faint sprint
Lethal, distinct
Abkhazian martial apprentice
Momentous in his acrimonious 8 ball
Pocketed acid wash
The top hats golden number
Bowler, fluttered by green
Ruby more, perished neigh
Tram by rail, maybe it'll be Manchester
Down ported I trod over the dead sea scrolls
The spirit of a saw blade, tight toothed
Frenzy of the midlands
I want a return
The city calls
An island of misfortune
Surrounded in forest
Further surrounded in urban-
Dis-
-ease
The cow…
The shotgun…
And the bucket of unshelled salt liberties.

How invested are you in jazz
It should have a capital J
I wish I could capitalise my mind
So others wouldn't
I'm the scapegoat of the mystical west
With my clay-newspaper
I miss the stories daily
They feel unnatural
To me and to read
Perfect day
I had no troubles to sweep away

I don’t call it God I call it faith of heart
I hallucinated a cat, update at 19:00
Its 16:15
I can’t take opiates now, i’m in too much pain
Functionalist society, i'm not german
I do dig bauhaus
Oh not 3 crates of heineken i’ll get bored
The thoughts of the benzi-drizzled maniac
No-drine
Drina flows through a bonus province on her way to salt
I’m embarrassed by how much i want chicken goujons
I want them to draw the outline of my dick, then slide me it after a show
Dont talk of religion

Hitler

Sinister, as I walk on by

Uninspired hangover
And bananas a quick fix
Stomach envelope knife
Or a dissolving branch
2 handles
2 units
I hope that is all
My system will cleanse
By accidental force
I swear by survival on cannabis
She understands
I don't feel like talking to anyone so I talk to myself
I am in ecstasy
It's on the only the devil that convinces me otherwise
Brews a saviour when I can speak straight
Abolition single malt
Twisters
Not even I know where
Call me if you need help
Don't...
I'll pass out.

Lindo girassol
Zapinjes (you're tripping)
Hot orange but it bites
Keep.
Warm.
Peels far from fine
Ponderosa oak sapped sycamore
Put my liver through a 4th world war
The 3rd being on my lungs and Palestine
I don't have medals to give out because of my socialist epigenetics
Im straighter for medium beige feet
Than ginsberg is gay for black dick
I don't know if he ever got it...
The light feet don't, got laid
Pondered pines
Do harddrives dream of data? Unstored...
My dad accidently touched a bible once.
Never again...
"Maybe I'm too stupid..."
You're not.
A kind old man gave me an accidental piece of advice.
Women are good at elaborating on small things.
Men can condense a lot into a few.

Thank you, green beanie'd gardener

Named Peter.

River hadn't found the band of travelling baboons yet, it's in the like mind but I don't liken yours to mine, placeholder characters in cup position cowboy try these characters aren't around I have to bring them to life
I'd quite like some tangierian haze if that's what they press into hashish
Do I start walking or do I go back to bed, I won't wake up by the gold in marrakesh either way
This coffee tastes like sauerkraut no matter how much I put down
As if more will improve the taste
Lebanese skull bone grindings into fine chalk paste powder
I feel like I'm at a British disco before closing with this song playing its blissful
Coffee no cocaine
Yes shame
Her eyes vowed Eddie hazel
Dreaming bay side bats from battersea to baton rouge
I need to steal a pen
I'm not paying a pound.

Your flat looks like a corby girls pussy after a crack nandos night on the old town just a community centre no bums derelict houses untorn I imagine it's where they warm the spoons n hardened blades drinking 8% because Temples favourite number is 8 I think for music only
I don't know what else he uses numbers for professional musicians gal-- gala not galactic galore Crosby led harmony out of the silent night
Holy freight
An awful sensation from my stomach as I think about my day ahead-I-forget it happens on its own.

Your soft notes
Calm me
The way my mothers did
When I was a child

Your soft notes care for me
When I can't see my own face

Your soft notes hum
In the background
As I try to get some rest

Don't turn your soft notes off...

I am being made

Thank you, Lindo…

Jerry's tone is heroin
is that 4 on the floor
Billy's skin
Mixolydian pin prick

Don't call me that
Im spiritual
I have mystical visions
And raise the...
I try to be sad but my eyes dry up
Can't I have my fun
Sa...
I only write poetry
High in beer gardens
The beers okay

I write the way I ride a bike
Half retarded San Andreas
Wide leg jeane'd brown eye...
No change for the cap
And I'll take a Michael Owen pin
As well

So hungover-over i'd rather be working,
5 hours in I want a burger and joint, beer, line, cigarette, another joint but only one pull because who smokes joints back to back, sometimes.
I need some therapeutic antioxidants
To get me through without stimming
Screeching with the alpha 'tism
Berret sat unstraight
Without a military patch
Pakistan cricket instead
The proper front line
Here's the first drink, in 30 minutes or so when I'm back from the shop. I hate that road. I really dislike this town but it is... Wh
... And a joint

One beverage or an extra side?
There's a spilled budweiser in my bag
I'll sip that
Frozen yoghurt in my water glass, I'm out the door, 0 degrees outside but I've saved £3, and I wanted frozen yoghurt as I missed my chance on new year's day, peckham, they even had more flavours in this one---I still get vanilla, it's nandos gravy...
I guess I didn't want a beer...good.

The budweiser was whole
Sounded more bukowski
"Spilled bud"
I did spill it on the ground
So there's that
So unhealthy you remind me of a microwave
I'd put you on 100% either way
Defrost- like a lack of thermal leggins
Swept under your bed
Russian swirls rather than a sheet
... Kurva
Scratches my thighs
I sleep in my thigh high thermal leggins
With the cowboy hat on my light

"How did you sleep with the light on?"

What light...

Who's this...

I need humbling
It's just not how my brain works man
I don't even want it to the work that way
It would be someone else
"I don't belong to any kind of group" he said, "no, me neither" dry response, it's cold but less when you know he's homeless, bump into him all the time, good guy, movie character like the way you talk to him, go in a shop, he disappears. I might put my clipper in my bum and take a picture just for that line, I'm not drunk enough or at all. I was gonna get some fast food but I gave the money to him instead and it's a win-win, I'm glad, satin ochre night, over Bedford, similar to that of luton but not as gloom though luton has a bigger sky overall, bigger horizon and better spots, better food, better crackheads, walk you home so gently, like an Egyptian tour guide in the old town of Hurghada "my brother owns a shoe shop come this way"
Other way
I couldn't walk faster if I tried, back in Luton in winter, those airport winds make the entire town freeze all the more
Drinking magnum wine and smoking haze is assimilating to the local culture around here, Lutonites will nod, I'll be going to Cambridge in the coming days to write, and when I was last there, on Ketamine, about half a gram throughout an afternoon, lost, happy christ felt moments no phone it was a true classic...

I had the best beer in my life and couldn't charge my laptop to find the bus stop, laptop for a bus stop, I know, been to Cambridge tonnes of times, lost. New canals and Floydian meadows with a singular cow, on a meadow, Portugal street made me laugh hysterically and it's a silly inside joke, typing Portugal in the chat of a csgo streamer, or a forum, usually all caps too, ohhh, nostalgia sweeter than a cigarette... Beer on a wooden surface aroma

High pitch female laughs, oh.

I'll deafen a little

I have

Thanks to jazz

I missed my timing for a perfect exhale, I'll have to wait, can't rush it, prefer leaning on things to smoke unless I'm indoors, it might just be a winter lean, you should have something to say.

Are poor people constantly in pain?

I know my back hurts when I don't smoke.

It's just me

Talking to myself

Empty cafe

Painful streets until you catch blue

Then green

Diffused

I watched mad Ricky see Christ then I saw him myself
Homeless Nike air, tear filled eyes
It wasn't music
He had no phones on
I could feel his peace
Reheat lunch it was nice
Ukulele hanging out
Head to toe in royal blue
Riding through town square
He just fits in
He used to patrol Queens park
Now Ampthill road
I used to think he was unconscious
When he's in a good mood he looks and laughs
Never exchanged a word
Mad Ricky
"Ain't so mad" the Canadian harmonica player said
"he's got a joint in one hand and a cider in the other...
And he's dancing"
He knows what he's doing
"Oh he knows"
Mad Ricky
Ain't so mad
I for one am certainly.

Going behind a bush to suck a lemon, I thought I was gonna get stabbed so I went home, didn't want the heavy load so a lemon and cigarette will do.
Running away to fold out my internal luggage, going to project on legally bound friends, taste of greggs while looking at aeroplanes from yellow bus windows Starbucks across. I don't want to go home yet and I've nothing to miss but rather...
Short cake brownie thing, nice with black coffee walking like a turkey off beat I love your glare i'm too high too care or really notice my rattling gatling gun of a restless leg while I sit on the train, electrified, yellow is now orange your station is closing the grey is falling off of the ceiling dust out of the fan my cigarettes want a refund as the most dangerous inhalant around wet rubber vinyl sticker ground bad pattern and feel for stains but great for drunken English legs o2 1am fools saloon I'm the fool for departing so late Londons a city without a remedy it's people talk and tweet while asleep
Not a Buddhist sleep a physiological one
That ones not up for interpretation
This one talks 3cm from your face uninterested she still laughs with vogue hysteria smell of south east postcode sweat with dirty nikes londoners don't dress up to go out but rather adjacent
Small bladder or a feeling for...

No, I only toke.

Watchers of doveless skies
Remembered why it came to be
Recent thoughts... memory
Trees turning to unhardened ware
Honey swirls drizzle down bark canals dearly-sickly sweet wept up the undue frenzy, London bricks unmortared as wires unsoldered or cut loose from deathly disorder, I would have warned you, if I could have sewn the cream linen covers, for the ambitious teens and childrenless mothers, skirt torn laid over shells, it's why damnation is a powerful word, there's a place in hell,
Angel of death I left my body but my spirit remains, it flutters from my skin to triads of alloys molten, unharmonised, no new tourniquet , it fades, grand illusion of mine
I blew the whistle before it was time
I'm now down to my last breath

Oh lady, please save me from my certain death.

Maize in an ashtray smoked chia mould never a name so fitting for the smell
Substituted blood for substance
Veins on radiator until the ice blows away
Animal of man
Act one way
Before the play resumes on its own
It was written on undue faith by a crystal shaman, selling tricks to elevate above rising dew, raising rains, growing...
The uni student bar had no ice cream so I left with a discounted coke and hand rolled cannabis cannon tucked in my female tight pockets, revealing above knit cardigan-argued to wear over my partner, it matched her hair, not her frame, I have a video game esc silhouette dollhouse pose so i made us breakfast that day as a trade for the cardigan, she liked my breakfasts, custom vostockian omelette or custom oats... I'll even walk to a cafe if you don't like my roast.
I hung my head, I remember when we didn't have enough money for rent, 23 miles for a charitable food shop, "£50, is this all we got"
And I couldn't-in-wit this one, but the lack of gratitude hurts, food is food when you have it, when you don't.
Hydrated and happy to be around is how I feel and I dig this fresh breathe
It's not smoke this time I'm not choking

Even the micro hairs that poke me in the eye don't bother the paragon of thought
Intuition stray by counting or not counting the breaths
I've lost it again and before I could finish the sentence---it's back

Old school high
I'm not drowning out thoughts
Give me your remedy
Who's clear to see?
Clear to provoke your inner God
Against the man at the imagined top
Human---not
This brush of vowels tickles my eyebrows
Tonight an unsad kind of night
Few too many edge rests for a man in a lifetime
I'll sit on the edge just one more time
What could it cost?
Fumbling Bowler hat off veridian with lilac kosh, Lily pad sewn in triple breastfed blazer I'll fitted like an lower school child, with a clip on tie, jumper get got shiny sheen reflecting brightly in jittery lights, creaking from horror, clock has frozen, my margins are full of faces in oceans, wondering what I'm here for...
Maths doesn't make sense so I'll let it not make sense
It occurs to me I've always been lost
I am not afraid of death
As if i've taken a car for a spin before
That's how I've always lived
Killer respawn
I was either a policemen or serial offender
Potentially a soldier with an ungodly scoreboard spree---eyes through glass zoomed in, a child a mother, which do I kill first and will the child get away?

I save all the cats, boss didn't tell me what to do and I only follow him, I lost all my thoughts in battle and they only comeback through PTSD on return, no real pension and I don't have a room but it was important to fight for my country, there's nothing I can learn, I'm more afraid than the children I'm frighting killing fucking so ridiculously bad, to know an average salary feeds killers makes it worse and you're worse than the worst fucking Jews controlling world views along with the news nothings new stop repeating it, headlines of reheated shit from a microwave and that's what you print on the retinas of the masses who read news as if it were truth, sticking to anything is gonna get you stuck people have lost balance with unsustainable diets that damage their precious climate and planet, animals they treat as toys, no walks, this dog evolved to hunt and retrieve and serve and you've got it on a lead indoors, working in British houses you observe the truest depression known and that's my own projection but that man should write a book and not I, I wouldn't have children if I was going to talk to them like that and to think I receive a kiss on my head from true wisdom, why are the people suffering?

I'm on the edge, like I've always been.
Boroughs was not a poet but a anal cavity excavator of young old black white not turning down the heroin... I guess he did come back from Tangiers, for the spectrum of white cock and brown balls but in American dream freedom. Boroughs a poet? Are teens romantics?
Smack grin take a drink with Jack, blow with Joe, you have to stop taking Lucy at some point or she turns on

you like a bright magenta devil in the rays of true beauty you cant turn it down it shows you the right and the lightness afterwards, you delve into the dark like a Knight protecting his... Princess? Or the king's throne, he likes defending a queen... Noble, it's read every which way... It's his bible, a fool's guide to spirituality is looking at the sky, then the trees whisper that the horizon is bit yet deep enough, it's just around the corner, hornets nest, frosted fruit in place of teas to cool, am I being cool or are you too cool? Impresses a fool
I am impressed
I am the fool
Pretending to contain other skies
My backgrounds only one
River was incredibly reclined when he uttered the line "if I wasn't to move I'd die this time tomorrow" Stylogram responded with great Heineken heat straight from pub warmed up plastic tray food
"What would kill you...if not I" in a great Shakespearean voicing, Stylopathy always made fun of my poetry with his silly Oh Romeo voice... No death down this Folkestone bridge alley, why would Chinese people go there, no photos only wind fish and green is there a sea creature itemised wind fish like this storm flower---already too late he's made happy hour covered in paint Tuesday work leg hurts kind of shake, I don't envy builders or the money they make---helps my spine feel like a spine as though it were a snake through skin, not tattooed---pierced Vlad the impaler kind, the only Vlad I know does cladding for pounds in change, dumb as a horse his wife says though a nice man, rolling

stones but I want Stan Getz, I keep thinking of microwaves yet I don't use them, 4th in 104 poems, kebabs shouldn't be microwaved but rather shawarma'd---it's fresher, where's it from I won't Google, grills better in the thinner pieces than meat fat slice hardened paste leg of visual desaturated spectrum ohhhh glorious only drunk but I mean drunk not 4 beer mediocrity of night I survive my blues in with joints in between cigarettes halfway between joint and beer...
Conversation happens all the time when the beat is booming alcohol splits attention when did you say it was a solo on dreamin wrong bpm but he steered it clear from the shore, the bald duck is boring I want a 23 year old with demons in her crotch and more in her closet
Charlie bird on jazz samba, which one is he?
I stumbled upon these melodies. Why do they deal?
I'm no angel

Demons reveal
I'm no...

I'm only surreal
Where did you get your last...?

Why did you steal?
The mosquito got bit that night

He went down in the foam of his precious pale ale

Is it easier to get up after a good night's sleep or horrific?
Nihilistic stanza
As my stomach metabolises another round of poison, even the server looked at me weird
Maybe I need to start hopping
Or skipping
Sitting with the old folks isn't rewarding
Free is free I won't pour it
I should have taken it then left like a hidden Tuesday Terrapin
What terrain did he fur with algae for seals to store salt
We've lost touch with our salty roots as well as mycelial
Pretending it's the government that's killing you
Oh...
Then why were they acting mysterious?

Lithium Ion
And a pack of bottled adrenochrome
Nonced throne sat

Abusing lost ill fostered youth
Child scent perfume
Epstein's private room
Stephen Hawking was there too
Disney land full of doom
Disney was always doom filled
Slavery at the point of sale
You better stay on site
Otherwise it doesn't count

I've been sleeping
By the ol clay pigeon
Just waiting to get shot
The post cards don't mean a happy thing
Lucky I got sent some smut
I won't just throw them out
My draws full of council poems
They say son,you better ACT NOW
I've been sleeping
Like an ol clay pigeon
Just waiting to get shot
My lucks a funny thing
It's either yin or it's yang
My parents didn't think I need a middle name
The taxi took river for a drive
Dylan Garcia
I gave my son a silly folk retainer
Maybe he'll sing in his father's bay
Don't drop dead please sweet River
Your middle phrase is not to blame
Motorboat was taken far out wide
I taught you to swim through a hurricane
Ozarks left dumbfounded when he swam out with a stolen face
Hey hey Father Timmy
I never drowned go file a case
My blood work is super clean sir
I can outpace goggins through a night
Don't tell me I drowned in 2nd place

Lover, you should've come over... Last night when the winds didn't howl your name.
If I drink then go walking
Oh lady aren't you gonna stop me
Numb n untired
I reach for your suffering
It don't tangle me
Terpenes of tangie
Fallen like lost perfume
The dresser was divided
I had no eye glass to draw the line
It wasn't arousing
Whiskey drinking woman kept me up so long the dry Jim bourbon dried in her throat
If you're going to be a crackhead at least do it on purpose
Reacting to sounds like Theo's 'tistic house mouse
Searching for a forbidden fruit among commonalities
I stepped wrong
The queen was disgusted
Tomorrow is gone
And I can't live today
Please come back
I used to be a romantic
I can't believe I'm buying condoms to fuck some whore with the ego in my nose
I'm the whore
... I pretend she's my muse

Misused stronger than my sexual trauma at 11 years old, I burn him in my dreams yet he's still forgiven... Just learn... Demon. I almost corrupted another soul lucky Lucy managed to let it go
She's my back up when times are bad
I won't give you my borrowed bike I've already lent it out again
And I'll walk where I please when I'm well in serotonin.

Up flinging I don't mind drinking alone
I enjoy orange essence it reminds of your sauron clit
I once bit
Salmon treat as if it's got cocaine in it,
Either way it was a sophisticated free for all, I did hear it's good for...
Drumming, a drum teacher told me, my childhood best friends dad---sober not much of it gooey God I'm in for an accidental social frenzy, I have no cards to play, don't even look this way the forehead
No foreword
The drinking man's sober blues no pill's for the duvet tomb lack hard Crystal I've no saline I've never been able to find it the cleavage don't mind it the clever glare I look around a pinted wall prince's best stuff is unreleased yet out on the Internet
How many pages is too many for a book someone might read it even if they don't it's a hell of a script I even woke up in it a raspberry her name but I could never really see a face it reminds me of that great traffic song lyric, someone else will come and take your place... Are you feeling alright... Just a beer to myself---why do people run down stairs in boots so heavy bow legged, what a lovely guitar tone but horrible song maybe I do need someone by my side either east or west I don't wanna lay or be laid on what is it in the decrepit minds of 22nd century gun arming kids kids it is kids not the adult saying kids

Is that screen pre-recorded?

No it happens to be a live feed of the interior of the pub,
You housed ape
I don't want your children and I'm glad I won't be raising those gremlins plastic slides and cocaine with Steve the mechanic I say fuck my cunt so much I might as well have one stevie nicks was a great singer but not the best sitara is my favourite singer...Cameron guitarist... Lilly drummer... Alex is my local doom but with emotion, soon he'll be a global doom Silas' photographs are fitting for my book. Maybe I'll commission them... I haven't been those places but he has gentle soul he's the beat he's not been beat he lives the beat beat is king new beat generation is in spring and also summer winter is a farce it's just colder I have chills thank you bar man high street cellar bar bouncer laughed at my outfit I like your tache all thin teens told me to dance how do you respond without being a fool or no fun or... I'm not dancing... I'm not responding what black lady dance did she mean she was black I don't tiktok so it might be content from the great teen abyss
This isn't jazz this isn't beat i'm the one being beat no it's experibeat... English grandmother from Dulwich---don't use the word hate...

Songs about a dog fart in a kimchi jar... How many minutes left I'd go for a cigarette but my obstructed view seat will get taken, this is a good band playing absolute mouldy yeast pussy tenerife shore

Good solo on 'fornia dreaming thank you for the correct bpm it's beat she missed the beat so she went around one more time.... Hotel california

Wrong fill still... Didn't play the solo excuse me this is dad commentary another beer

This is a horror show I could smoke 21 cigarettes tonight yet I've only got 4 more and 4 people love losing their voices talking over live music

God this is a horrible flavour of waste at least the beer is to taste not kraft esc mac n cheese which I also enjoy

Men dance like autistic crabs not caught in cages, every song is 2 minutes shorter than the original thankfully

I love a place with visible metal tubing it's really classy I find

I'd rather be at... Taxi I want to go home no wait look at the space you are in 1959 in 2159, 2 days no alcohol and I return with a vengeance for sex and violence no no bombs I'm done with hearing about it please stop I can't repost your social bullshit i feel bad my people were under attack as if my people are different to people in general but it affected me so... Very superstitious.

I don't pay attention to dancing blonde girls I'm not a baboon

His hoodie covers his square glasses like a windshield damn she's cute... No... The beers... Wait the notes are coming out of my phone case is that a beat flex or a nitty crime I don't care I don't play cricket I think it's for losers

People act as though they are professionals when they move out of the way for someone carrying something quite English with the smug smirk it's not smug I'm just not overly British

I'm not walking on sunshine but some tar might help where's cameo

I want to go to Tangiers

What did Al see there

Or boroughs

If he thought not to return

I go to the smoking area outfront, a bummy looking individual carrying a case of Stella's and "can you call my phone... I lost it"

Where would it be were on the streets

I'm Larry

Do you know who I am

Shut your mouth when I'm talking to you

Watch your mouth do you think I'm a pussy hole my name is Larry you want to fight I'm a boxer you want a fight out there if you want a fight my rings out there I'm a bare knuckle boxer

Look what you've done

Pissy tissue for snot
That's why they call it rock n roll
Guys trying to seem interested making THAT face
No chance
She swims
Non foam waters for your kind
Out
You just know how to talk
How good
Ram on
I wouldn't waste my time if I were you I've already forgotten myself
I can't remember his name he was alright I'm not gay though imagine a dick poking you not in your eye
Just 2 days off and a drink again and I'm sick
Fuck your spirits
I was drinking beer
There's no vagina near and I have no anxiety
It just hurts
Fuck my cunt are you beautiful
I would make sex dolls of you and keep them to myself
Of course
Girls are funny your not in control neither am I
Denied
Denial
Fuck the skeletons in your closet by the cocacola cans and broken umbrellas.

Warren's a funny guy more than a doorman I feel like a drunk girl talking to the bouncer but not flirting but because I have no friends
Does anyone have friends?
Where does your faith come from?
Would it falter if I murdered your mother?
Pink hues induce serotonin
Particularly in flowing waters
Fish's bubbles
Uncatched hooks
Releasing air to the sky
Thanks for the smile
It made my day...
Synthetic rosary counting
I couldn't even think
How much I was writing
I couldn't even feel
How much I was thinking
I'll take a moment
16:54
20 minutes and then 10 minutes later than before but still 4?
And again but 04:21
Alfie says he likes 8
Weird lei cat
Read me that poem...
My feet are underwater somewhere in this world

Clinton is a vegan
Vegans don't fuck—do they?
Congratulations on your misfortune
Now pay the Bill
Pussied cigar
For the canned tuna Febreeze
Who are you gonna find for your Caddington mortgage
I'm cold
But in a heated room
I get up
Only because the sun comes through
And then a joint
And I thank jesus for being born
It's been too long
Alder buckthorn
My favourite cigarettes are the cheapest ones
Marlboro---
Off you go...
As my grandma gives me more marlboro
I love asking a girls name then not asking her boyfriends
Duality
I need to get the gays off me
I've no siren or flag
That I'm a vagina man.

Unmetered poetry porn continues---Prose, as soon as set down, always in navy and brown and a pop punk of my own self
Where are the edgy folk and why am I not with them, tapping along to staying alive---crime filled hive mind, surrounded in disappointment bliss I love disappointment because my life's too good and predictable otherwise
There are more dead people than alive
Wonder what his name could be and who he's with, Jane goodall,
I feel sick at British troll women where are the Latina miracle whips
Start the show I haven't got all night long
Bubbles keep popping and I want to rock my head
Pop music is a virus at better times
It's like a tick to a council slug
Pocahontas provocation
Not on this side of the sphere
Tartan patchwork you give off Irish gay

Blue through grey
So devastatingly crude and bor-slab
From Slough or Coventry
Birmingham new street Richard Lewis-not comic saving suicidal souls or was it falling,
This night will not have been worth it if I don't get my chilli chicken goujons

And vegan v...
How does one find love in a hopeless place?
Is it on the map like glasses on face falling from hinge---suited apparently, left to dangle
Looking through the floor-blues
Listening to shit rather than playing good
I play too fast for what I enjoy but my receptors take it like a tactile drug
I thought that was a swastika tattoo
Luckily it's just misshapen pubes
I write more to notes than speak to human correspondence---sad
Pubs are for lonely men
Especially those coming with women.
Crackhead with a suitcase where you going
You're already under a bridge
Aren't you sleepy?

Taxi…I want to go home.

Printed in Great Britain
by Amazon

38527842R00142